THE FOLLY

THE FOLLY

Gemma Amor

POLIS BOOKS

The following is a work of fiction. Names, characters, places, events and incidents are either the product of the author's imagination or used in an entirely fictitious manner. Any resemblance to actual persons, living or dead, is entirely coincidental.

ISBN 978-1-957957-35-7
eISBN: 978-1-957957-47-0

Library of Congress Control Number: available upon request

First hardcover edition December 2023 by Agora Books
An imprint of Polis Books, LLC
62 Ottowa Road South
Marlboro, NJ 07746
www.PolisBooks.com

POLIS BOOKS

ONE

He shuffled out of the prison door in a daze, a small bag of belongings clutched to his chest. I saw him pause as the early light of day embraced him. He closed his eyes briefly, and dragged in a deep, full breath, up through his nostrils, out through his mouth. I had haggled for his release to be set at five in the morning, to help us avoid attention from the press. I had not accounted for how surreal exiting into an empty, quiet street must have felt for him. Like exiting onto the moon after a long flight.

The sky overhead was drenched in pink fire that morning, bright streaks of blue raking through. The prison walls, tall, thick, built of Victorian red brick, caught the weird dawn glow and hung on to it. It gave the complex a surreal, artificially lit aspect, as if it were a movie set or a paint and canvas creation, not the brutal bricks-and-mortar structure that had stolen my father for six and a half long years.

Prison had not been kind to Dad. That release day, I could not believe how much older than his true age he looked. Of course, I had visited him every week while he was inside, but now he was out, I could see clearly how diminished he was. White-haired, he stooped, which didn't suit him. My father had always been a straight-backed sort of man, a man who had once been proud of his height. Now he moved as if he were an inconvenience, as if he were actively trying to lessen the amount of space he took up in the world. He was thin, too, cheeks saggy. I was glad I had a shepherd's pie waiting for him at home, calorie-dense, smothered in cheese. I had made an apple tart for dessert, which I would serve with custard or clotted cream, or both, depending on how hungry he was.

Dad took a few more hesitant steps across the carpark. I went to him. We had been apart for a long time. I didn't want to waste another second.

"Hello, Dad," I said, gently taking his bag. It wasn't heavy, but he was having a difficult time with it. His arms shook. I swallowed back tears. My heart was pounding. I was determined not to cry in front of him. He had enough to deal with. He didn't need my sentimentality on top of everything else.

"Hello, love," he replied in a gravelly voice. "You didn't have to come get me. I could have got a taxi."

I shook my head, wondering when he would hug me. "With what money?" I scolded. "Come here." I could see he wasn't going to make a move, so I made it for him, wrapping him in a tight embrace. He stiffened at first, then slowly returned it. I drank in his smell, which I had nearly forgotten. Bones dug into me through his clothes. I estimated he'd lost at least thirty pounds, maybe more. He didn't feel like my dad, not yet, but he would soon enough. I would make sure of it.

We leaned into each other for a minute, then broke apart.

"Right then," I said, clearing my throat. "Let's get out of here, shall we? Before the media shows up."

"Yes, please," he replied, and I could see ghosts in his eyes.

Two

Dad's sentence had originally been a fifteen-year sentence. He served just over six of that, give or take thirteen months, which we both begrudged. I had hoped the furious media interest in his appeal and retrial would expedite his release, but, if anything, it had slowed things down. Bureaucracy, paperwork, logistics... the system wanted to hang on to him, an innocent man. A victim of a miscarriage of justice, although the press wouldn't communicate it that way. Dad's trial had been a trial of public opinion. It had not taken me long to learn that the truth, the real truth, as far as anyone could ever know it without having been present, was nowhere near sensational enough to drive clicks and sell papers. Accidents didn't make money, murder did. The best I could hope for now was a version of events that meant we could live our lives together again in peace, lives that had been disrupted beyond all belief after a simple trip, a split-second tumble. I tried not to feel angry about how things had gone, although I was. I was angrier than I knew how to cope with, but I squashed it down. Anger wasn't useful. Patience, I had found, was the only useful virtue. And acceptance. True, my family life had imploded in the space of an hour, but now...I had my dad back. That was all that mattered. Now was the time to look forward, not back. I could change none of the past.

I could change our future, though, for the better.

"There are still a lot of forms to fill out," I told him, putting the car into reverse and awkwardly three-point turning in the narrow street outside the prison. An approaching car barreling in the opposite direction jerked to a halt and honked, the driver motioning for me to hurry up. I waved back calmly. City drivers were all bluster, nothing more. The trick was not to back down, not to show that they had gotten to you.

"And we have a lot to discuss," I continued, eventually pointing us in the right direction and letting the other car squeeze past aggressively. Our wing mirrors clipped. Dirty looks were exchanged. The other car's exhaust belched and roared, and the vehicle sped off. Just another encounter in a world full of aggravation and stress, par for the course for the times. The pandemic had brought out the very worst in people, I thought, but I didn't say so to my father.

I pulled away from the prison for what I hoped would be the very last time. I felt as if I knew every aspect and contour of the place, every brick and slab. I hated it.

Dad, meanwhile, watched the building grow smaller in the rearview mirror.

"You know," he said quietly, "I've waited so long for this moment, and now it's here, I'm afraid."

"Afraid of what?"

"Everything. All of it." He waved a hand at the world passing slowly by: shuttered shops covered in graffiti, cafes, bakeries, vomit-splattered bus stops, greengrocers, pubs with tables and chairs stacked atop each other on the path outside, a church, a supermarket, pound stores, designer boutiques, estate agent offices, second-hand furniture stores—a relentless commercial jumble, a chaotic urban kaleidoscope that must have been a lot to absorb after the sparse and spartan world of prison. Even if it was all closed doors, now. To me, it felt like a zombie town. The city had been in lockdown for so long it was hard to remember what life had been like before. For Dad, though, it must have been a siege upon the senses.

"Want me to put you back in?" I joked, although the joke hurt my heart. "I could drop you off in time for lunch."

He chuckled, just one short burst of hard-won mirth, then hung his head as if he did not deserve to laugh. I could almost see the hefty mantle of guilt sitting heavily on his shoulders as he began to process his freedom. He didn't feel he deserved it, even if it had been granted by law. He had been so conditioned to his own worthlessness inside, it would take time to reprogram him as a blameless man, I knew. Patience would be necessary. We would have to rebuild him, brick by brick, from the ground up. It wouldn't be quick or easy, but time would play its part. And space to breathe. Peace. Fresh air. A change of scene.

I had a plan for all of that.

He could sense my mood, in that intuitive way he'd always been able to with me.

"You don't have to do all this, you know," he said, patting my hand as it rested on the gear stick. "You don't have to put me up. I can find my own way. My own place."

"I'm not so sure about that."

He shook his head. "A parent should look after his child, not the other way around. Not at your age."

I shook my own head in mild exasperation. "At my age? I'm pretty sure most people my age are looking after at least one parent, if not both. You aren't a spring chicken anymore, Dad. This is how it works, isn't it? It's why people have children."

He sighed. "That cynical brain came straight from your mother, didn't it."

I pursed my lips. "Don't. I can't, not today."

"You know what I mean. I should be able to look after myself."

"And you would live where exactly? You know how difficult it will be to get a job. Especially at the moment. People are losing their jobs left, right, and centre. And it'll be a nightmare trying to get insurance. *And* you don't have the money to rent, you lost all your savings."

"Jobseeker's allowance," he muttered, a little cowed. "Universal Credit."

"Those will only get you so far in this city. Do you know how expensive it is to rent these days? You want to live in some mouldy old hovel with a bunch of addicts? Or a tent in the centre of town? Camp out in the Bearpit? Stop being silly. You're my dad. Of course you're going to live with me."

"I could, you know. Put myself back in. Commit another crime. Find a police officer, assault them. That's a thing, you know. Some of us get so used to being inside that we walk right up to the first copper we can find after release and—"

"Dad!" I was horrified, for he sounded half serious.

"I could. Then I wouldn't be any bother."

"Dad, stop it. We fought for this, for years. You're

free now. Free to live your own life. I'm just helping you get back on your feet is all."

Dad was silent as he pondered the word *free*.

"I suppose you're right," he said eventually.

"Now, stop spoiling things. This is a day to celebrate! I have a hot meal waiting for you at the house. A freshly made bed. Let's get you away from town and settled in. Then we can talk properly."

"Shepherd's pie?" he asked, meek and humble, a mode I never liked that much in him.

I smiled. "Of course. Your favourite. Just the way Mum used to make it."

He thought about it. "Got any beer?"

I smiled. "A celebratory bottle of Tribute, and your favourite glass."

He sighed. "You're a good girl, Morgan," he said. Then: "It will be nice to see the old house again. I've missed my home."

I kept quiet. He didn't know yet that it wouldn't be his home for much longer.

THREE

Heavy with food and ale, we both studied the tabletop. Empty plates scraped well clean lay stacked in a neat pile between us. Dad was itching to wash them, I could tell. He had been conditioned to organise, to clean, to put things away. I noticed that immediately on his return to our house. He had taken off his shoes, placed them tidily on the shoe rack, then meticulously unpacked his small bag of possessions and rearranged his room so it looked not that dissimilar to how I imagined his cell had looked. All extraneous clutter pushed firmly under the bed, out of sight, so surfaces were clean and bare. His clothes, folded precisely and placed in order of colour in his chest of drawers. It would take some getting used to, this neatness. Before,

Mum had done all these things for him. She had scolded him about mess, clutter, and untidiness repeatedly. It had never been a question of laziness or malice: he simply hadn't seen the disorder or disarray in those days. He had been oblivious to most chores until they were pointed out to him. Mum used to complain that he would not tie his own laces until she told him they needed tying.

Prison had changed all that.

Now that the eating was done, his face had a hectic, flushed look that alarmed me a little. I hoped he could keep his food down. What a waste it would be otherwise. I thought perhaps I shouldn't have prepared such a rich, calorific meal, but I'd wanted to mark the occasion properly. An old boyfriend had once told me I expressed love with food, and I supposed he was right. Food and love, love and food. "You'll love me into a new pair of trousers, Morgan," he'd said. I'd taken that as a compliment.

I mentally shook myself. Remembering that relationship hurt too much. Instead, I imagined the ingredients in the pie I'd prepared coursing through Dad's malnourished body: the best lamb mince, the freshest vegetables, homemade beef stock, and home-grown tomato sauce.

Would it be enough to soften the blow of the news I had?

I looked at him, so frail, so thin, so bowed. I didn't have the heart to tell him, not today.

Conversation in general, it turned out, would prove remarkably difficult with Dad post-release. This was something I had not anticipated. Neither of us had spoken for nearly an hour beyond the necessities of eating dinner—*pass the salt, would you like water, I hope it isn't too hot.* We weren't used to each other in such large doses. And at first, that was okay. At first, I left him to it. I thought perhaps he didn't want to talk to me because he was tired, overwhelmed.

But the silence dragged on, and on, became painful. Eventually, I figured out that I shouldn't take it personally. It was just that a man who had been locked away in a small room for years on end with no job, no hopes, no dreams, and no friends probably didn't have much to talk about. It would be down to me to make conversation, not him. I had a life. He didn't.

So, I said:

"We need to get some more clothes for you, but it's hard with all the shops shut. Thank god for the internet, eh?"

He grunted. I'd chosen the one thing to discuss that he knew nothing about. He didn't have a phone or a laptop, didn't care about social media. He'd not needed to before prison. He and Mum had kept plenty busy. Holidays, work, hobbies. They'd been part of a large circle of friends. Those friends had now dispersed, like seeds on a breeze. Mum had been the glue. Her death: social acetone, dissolving the niceties of bingo and poker nights with extreme efficacy. Afterward, not a single one of them wrote to Dad. Nobody wanted to associate with a murderer. It wasn't the done thing in our neck of the woods.

"Want me to cut your hair?" I asked, needing to get my mind on something less dreary.

Dad ran a hand over the uneven mess on top of his head.

"If you like," he said quietly.

I fetched the clippers from the bathroom, draped a towel around his shoulders. He sat stoically while I gave him a close-cropped buzz. Hair dropped to the floor all around, landed on his shoulders. He itched at the sharp strands that escaped down his shirt collar, and I slapped his hands away multiple times.

"What's this?" I said once I was down to the scalp. "This is new." A scar marked the back of Dad's skull. Thick tissue in the shape of something curved. He'd been hit with a blunt object, I realised.

"I had a falling out with my cellmate," he replied quietly.

I said nothing, but dropped a kiss onto the top of Dad's head. "Go make yourself a drink," I told him, gathering the towel from around his shoulders in a way that stopped any more hair dropping to the floor. "You've earned it."

On my way out the front door to shake out the towel, I passed the spot where it happened. The accident. Not that anyone could tell now. I'd painted over everything, but sometimes, if the light hit in a certain way, I imagined I could still see her blood, shockingly red.

I stepped around the area, like I always did, an awkward, staggering side hop to avoid walking where she had fallen.

When I came back inside, I found Dad sitting on the top of the stairs, staring down at the redecorated patch. He had a drink in one hand, a scotch and soda, and he was swirling the ice in it with the index finger of his free hand. His face was lost to memory. I looked up at him, but he didn't see me.

I let him sit. There wouldn't be many more opportunities for him to do so, after all.

A good thing, for both of us, I thought.

FOUR

Another day, another dinner. Shepherd's pie again. I thought it might soften the blow.

I chose after the meal to drop the news. He responded to things better when he wasn't hungry.

"It's in Cornwall."

"Cornwall?" I could tell it would take a while to sink in.

"Well, I didn't think you'd want to stay around here, not after...everything."

He stared at me. "What would make you think that?"

I gestured in the general direction of the hallway, where Mum had died. I didn't need to elaborate beyond this. I barreled on.

"Anyway, I need a change of scene, even if you don't.

I can't stay in this house anymore. Not with the memories everywhere."

We both looked at the large colour photograph of Mum framed on the far kitchen wall. The glass in the frame needed a clean: grease and dirt had built up without me knowing it. I felt momentarily embarrassed about that, but Dad didn't seem too upset.

I went to the photo, took it down, started to polish the glass with a tea towel. A distraction. Neither of us were fooled by it.

"But this is our home," Dad said. He sounded exhausted. I wondered when his last night of good sleep had been.

"There's a saying about that, isn't there?" I countered. "Home is where the heart is. Well, my heart has gone out of the place, Dad, if I were to be brutally honest with you. I can't walk past the bottom of the staircase without…" I trailed off, not wanting to hurt him more than I already had.

Too late. He flinched and started picking at his fingernails. I stopped polishing, put out a hand to still his anxiety.

"It just doesn't feel like a home to me anymore. It feels like a time capsule."

I told him this as gently as I knew how.

He didn't like hearing it.

"Don't say that, Morgan. You grew up here. You were born here. Your mother…"

He fought to continue.

"It's just another thing I have spoiled for you," he finished, with difficulty.

"You haven't spoiled anything, Dad." I knew this was hard for him, but I wasn't giving up. "I'm forty-three years old. I've never lived anywhere other than my childhood home. Does that sound right to you? It doesn't to me."

"We liked having you here, with us. You were never a burden."

"That's not the point." I knew I was right, and besides. It had all been arranged. At this juncture, talking about it was a courtesy, for we were moving whether Dad liked it or not.

"Well, what *is* the point?" He was struggling with anger now.

"It's not just the house," I replied, trying to make it easier on him. "It's everything. I'm tired of the city. Of the noise. Before the virus…some days I couldn't move down the street for people and the traffic pollution. It's fine now, but when things go back to normal…" I shook my head, studied Mum's face behind the glass. Her hair, long, wavy, thick, and shiny as a chestnut, framed her features in a dense brown cloud. When she watched television or read a book, she would twirl one long strand of it through her fingers obsessively, over and over, a sort of calming ritual. I had picked up the habit not long after she died, and as soon as I'd caught myself twirling my own thin lustreless mousy hair through my own fingers, I'd taken Dad's clippers to my head, cropped it as close to my scalp as possible, and kept it like that ever since. It was easier, anyway, to manage. More practical. That's what I told myself on the days where I found my hand going to the side of my head, searching for something to work with.

Nearly seven years without Mum, and the grief still felt like a new wound. It ached, and I needed to get away from that, if I could. Far, far away.

"I need fresh air," I said. "Countryside. Better food. It's by the sea, you know, this place. You'll be able to take walks every day, and it's remote. Hardly any people around to bother us."

"You ashamed of me, then?" he replied with some effort.

I stared. "God, no," I said eventually. "How can you ask me that? It's not about hiding away. I just thought, after everything, that you'd want a fresh start. Privacy, especially after being in…that place." I hung Mum's picture back up on the wall where it belonged. "And it's not as if you have that many options, is it?"

I didn't mean this as unkindly as it sounded, or perhaps I did. My feelings about Dad, now that he was living with me again, were confused, but I had expected that. It was just a matter of adjusting to a new rhythm. I'd been on my own for so long it was hard to be around anyone else this much. I'd get used to it. Anyway, I was sure Dad had heard a lot worse in prison. And the quicker he understood that we were moving, and soon, the better.

He chewed on my statement, silently picking shepherd's pie from between his teeth. They were in a bad state, I could tell: his gums bled profusely and one of his incisors had a crack in it that I could see from where I stood. I resolved to register us with a dental practice in Cornwall as soon as I could. As soon as they opened for business again. Along with the rest of the world.

What a life, I thought, in which every basic human need had become a protracted operation. Grocery shopping, doctor appointments, dentist appointments, haircuts, all the everyday shit we'd taken for granted suddenly layered with anxious complexity. What a world for Dad to come out into, after everything he suffered already. It didn't feel fair, but I knew it couldn't last. Which brought me back to patience, and the virtue of it.

With that in mind, I kept quiet, letting Dad come to terms with things at his own speed.

Dad belched and scratched the top of his head as he thought it over. All these little tics he had picked up in prison: scratching, picking, worrying. It would drive me mad, I knew it, if he carried on like that. I would have to find something for his hands to do that was not self-destructive.

He arched his back, made an uncomfortable face. His cheeks were flushed again. He was full, overly so. I had kept him in that state since his return home. He hadn't complained about it, not once.

"They know about my conviction? They don't mind?"

Steering my mind back to the matter at hand took effort, but I managed it.

"The man I have been speaking to works with the local council on prison reform campaigns. He has a number of places around Cornwall. Makes a habit of employing ex-cons. Rehabilitation, he calls it. He knows all about you."

Under the glass, Mum's eyes watched us. She seemed sterner than she had for a while. Was she struggling with having Dad back, too? Or did she disapprove of my plans?

"What are your intentions for this place, then?" My father echoed my thoughts and gestured to our house, our home.

I hadn't told him yet that the money expected on the sale of the house would be immediately eaten up by the astronomical legal fees Dad's retrial had incurred. I didn't want to tell him either. Money had always been a flashpoint for Dad. Knowing I was insolvent would burst his banks. Yet I found I didn't mind being destitute as much as I knew I should, for it had been for the best of reasons.

"Sell it," I said, not wanting to dwell on that side of things too much.

"What if I don't want to sell it?"

Poor Dad.

"I have power of attorney," I replied gently but firmly.

"Oh," he said, his face drooping with sadness. "Is that how it's going to be?"

"For a while," I confirmed. "That's how it has to be."

There was no further argument after that.

FIVE

Graves were a lot of work, when all was said and done. They needed constant maintenance: trimming grass so it didn't grow tall and obscure the gold lettering you paid such an extortionate amount of money for, wiping off bird droppings, throwing away dead flowers and replacing them with fresh ones, at first, every week, then every few weeks, then only on special occasions like Christmas and Easter and birthdays. The day we left Bristol was the latter for Mum. Had she lived, she would have been sixty-four years old. She always used to joke about how she would never see her seventies, and that suited her just fine. "I don't want to get old," she told me repeatedly. She got her wish, although I spent the rest of my life wondering how things would have been if she hadn't.

We stopped at the cemetery on our way out of town, the car loaded down with what little we owned. Dad said he wanted to lay flowers, and I bought us two bunches of mustard-yellow tulips on the way, but when we got to the site, he seemed reluctant. He had an odd expression on his face as he looked down at the mound of grassed earth capped with the polished granite cross, and I realised he had not seen Mum's grave yet. He had not been to her funeral. He had been in custody or prison for every part of her formal farewell from the world.

The last time he had seen her, she had been lying in a pool of blood at the bottom of the stairs.

I put a hand on his shoulder. "Bit of a shock?" I said, because I had felt the same when I watched her coffin lower slowly into the large rectangular hole in the ground. It had felt, in that moment, as if someone had shoved a hard hand into my chest and gripped my heart, making a cold fist with it, twisting and squeezing the joy out of me in slow, brutal increments. It hurt more than anything I had ever experienced, but I knew at the time that the pain was important, I knew it was useful. I supposed that was why funerals were essential: they presented our brains with a complete finality and a truth that was impossible to shy away from. Mortal remains were just that. They were not statements one could easily argue with, and when the first handful of soil hit the coffin lid on that rainy afternoon years ago, I had felt a door close inside me. That part of my life, I knew, was now over. The part where I could ring Mum any time of the day from wherever I was and ask her a question, no matter how serious or innocuous, knowing she would always answer, as if she were waiting by the phone for my call, because I rarely had to let it ring more than twice before she picked up. For a while after she died, I still rang the house whenever I was out and about, even though I lived there, because she had set up an answering machine service on the landline. When I called, it went through to the recorded message, and it was like terrible magic, listening to her voice after she had died. I could hear her speaking any time I wanted to, just by picking up the phone. Like I had a direct line to the afterlife. As if death had forgotten that one, small device bridging the past with my present.

Then, like the hair twiddling, I saw how unhealthy the constant calling was. I erased the message, reprogrammed the answering machine. Doing so had been another necessary step toward acceptance. Mum was gone, and her end had been a painful, violent one, and no amount of listening to her cheerful greetings on the answering machine was going to change that. The only way was onward, I knew this. The funeral, the answering machine...all of it was there to show me that the state of death was final, no matter how hard I wished it weren't.

Dad, however, had not had any of those moments. He had been staring at four bare walls with only the image of his blood-splattered, crumpled wife for company. So it was no surprise, I thought, that he was struggling to lay yellow flowers on her grave. It probably didn't even feel like she was down there, because he only had my word for it that she was.

Perhaps that made me the luckier of the two of us, for I'd had plenty of time to get used to the idea.

I loosened my tulips from their plastic and laid them in a bunch on the mound. I thought this would prompt movement from Dad, but it didn't. He just stood there, those hollow eyes fixed on the headstone.

Come on, Dad, I thought, with some desperation. *Snap out of it. I need a parent right now. I need a father.*

Instant shame followed the thought, for his pain must have been unfathomable in that moment. I knew this, but it was hard to control my own feelings as we stood staring down at Mum's grave. My shame and guilt were suddenly replaced with the ever-nagging sense of frustration that was fast becoming a personality trait instead of an occasional inconvenience.

Because he wasn't the only one having a hard time, was he?

But then I forced myself to think of it from his perspective. How traumatised he must be.

And then I swung back the other way, a sentimental volte-face I could barely keep up with as my thoughts raced.

But he wasn't the only one. He wasn't.

When Dad had been sentenced, I had been orphaned, practically and emotionally, at a much younger age than I had anticipated being parentless. I had been thrust into a new phase of life, a lonely phase, an unguided phase, which was both terrifying and oddly liberating. I had begun to explore this strange new freedom in small ways: rearranging the furniture in the house, away from where Mum would have placed things, knowing she would have hated the nesting coffee tables being at right angles to the couch instead of placed squarely in the middle of the living room, but understanding it was important for me to place my own mark on the place, knowing that I had long put off having any sort of personal freedom because I had been seduced by this notion of family, of intimacy, of...

None of these thoughts were helpful. Being in the cemetery was sending me into a downward spiral. I needed to get away, and quickly, before it was too late.

"Put the flowers down, Dad," I commanded as softly as I could. "There's a vase right there." I could not stand in this graveyard any longer than I absolutely had to, reminiscing about the day I had scrubbed Mum's blood off the hall walls, repainted them buttercup yellow, poured the last dirty remnants of her down the sink in a pinkish swirl. I did not want to think about how alone I had been, how scared, how rudderless. I did not want to think about any of that. I just wanted to get on the road and drive, onwards to the sea.

Dad sighed and unwrapped the flowers. I helped him to cut the plastic zip tie strangling the stems and arrange them in the stone jar at the foot of the cross. It had a water reservoir in it, with a metal cap punctured with holes to keep the flowers tidy. I found that stupid cap the most depressing part of Mum's grave, although I could not have explained why.

Duties done, we stood side by side in silence, listening to the wind in the trees that circled the cemetery, staring at the piled earth, and I tried hard not to think about what condition Mum's mortal remains were actually in after all these years. It was tough to stop the brain from pursuing that line of enquiry, given the purpose of the turned soil in front of us. I glanced at Dad, and could see him working through a million different feelings, unable to settle on any particular one for any length of time.

"Come on, then," I said, trying to make a move.

"Do you think she's comfortable down there?" he asked in a cracked voice.

I resisted the urge to throw my arms up in exasperation.

"Dad, it's a grave, it's not going to be anything for her, comfortable or otherwise. She can't feel pain anymore, remember?"

"I know. But I mean...do you think...?" He stopped, wiped a hand across his eyes. "I know this sounds stupid, but do you think her bones are comfortable? She liked to sleep in a certain way, you know. She was particular about how she lay herself down."

And there it was again, the image of her body, creased and bloodied, invading my mind. Neck, horribly twisted. Red, seeping into the carpet beneath her, running down the walls, splattered across the stair bannisters. Limbs disorganised. An untidy end. Dad was right: she had been particular about how she lay herself down, Mum had always been a very neat and tidy sort of person. Her messy death hurt all the more for knowing that.

Would I ever get her final shape out of my mind? She had looked as if she were playing at death at a murder-mystery cocktail party. It had all seemed so unnatural.

I placed a hand on his shoulder and gave it a gentle squeeze. I was being selfish, and I needed to stop, for both our sakes. I forced myself to be kind, instead. In kindness, I found strength. Mum had been kind, after all. Unfailingly so. The least I could do was carry that tradition on.

"I made sure of it, Dad. They were very good at the funeral parlour. Her bones are comfortable. I promise."

He nodded, wiped his eyes again, and then once more when they refused to stop leaking, and then his shoulders erupted into heaving, pained sobs, and it struck me that he had not cried for Mum in prison, and this was years and years of grief, stored up, a blocked pipe now unplugged, and he needed to let it all out instead of being rushed off to a new life, so I took a seat under a cherry tree nearby and watched as he cried himself dry, and all around me, small pink petals drifted down like snow as the wind shook the trees of the dead gently and insistently, much like I wanted to shake Dad. But I didn't. I just sat there and let him weep it all out.

Half an hour later, he walked back to me. "We can go now," he said, and his voice sounded a little lighter.

"Sure?"

"I'm sure."

Neither of us would ever return to the cemetery again.

Six

It took roughly five hours to drive from the city to our new home on the Cornish coast, not far from a town called Newlyn. To get there, we followed the road through Exmoor National Park, along the Devon coastline and down past Tintagel until we got to Hayle, then cut across the tip of the country until we were almost as far south as we could go without landing in the Celtic Sea. It was the not the quickest or most direct route, but it was the prettiest. The drive was equal parts spectacular and frustrating, for the scenic routes were always the slowest, the roads more poorly maintained.

As we got closer to our destination, our journey took us past tiny fishing village after tiny fishing village, each of them shrouded in a thick sea mist that seemed to boil up out of nowhere despite it being sunny and clear further inland. Many of the places we drove through or around had tidal harbours as their main feature, harbours enclosed by granite breakwaters that curved out around them like protective arms, built to protect the town and its fishing fleet from the worst breakers that rolled in off the sea during storms, of which there were many in this part of the country. The breakwaters were capped with reddish-grey coping stones that reminded me of the curved bricks capping the top of the prison walls back in the city. Built in the same era, for a similar purpose, I supposed: to hold things back from the ordinary, everyday folk just going about their lives. Criminals and waves, murderers and crashing white horses woven from salt, the thought process was the same: keep away, keep away.

The tide was out for much of our drive, leaving behind many small curved moons of muddy sand with fishing boats pulled up high on them, listing over as if sleeping, waiting for the encroaching sea to eventually seep back in and float them upright again. We saw small children ducking in and out of green-slicked anchor chains stretching the length of each harbour, poking the sand between boats with sticks whilst seagulls cruised overhead. Each inlet was overlooked by rows of compact seafront houses laid along tiny winding streets that had not changed much since their original construction hundreds of years prior. Pubs that could have doubled as the setting for many a nautical romance novel dotted these harboursides: low-ceilinged, wooden beamed, with painted wooden signs and tiny windows, they were places where time stopped, atmospheric haunts once frequented by smugglers and pirates and fishermen, who, like their vessels, were waiting for the weather or the tide. All closed, obviously. The pubs had been some of the last businesses to shut their doors during lock-down, only admitting defeat when forced to do so by the government.

Despite the pandemic strangeness, they felt familiar, these seaside scenes. I supposed holidays as a child had left an imprint of recognition on me, a feeling that grew stronger the more I drove. I had a peculiar, gathering sense of both belonging and returning to something I hadn't realised I'd missed.

We saw few locals to begin with, aside from the odd hardy pensioner wandering across the road in front of us aimlessly, defiant of lockdown rules. That changed as we traveled further south. People were tired of being in their houses, that much was clear, and I didn't blame them. They needed air and light and space, just like I did. Flashes of rule-breaking went by our car windows with increasing rapidity. An old woman sat on a low wall overlooking the sea, drinking coffee and tugging on a cigarette as a gaggle of grandchildren clustered around licking home-made ice lollies. A cluster of cyclists clad in matching Lycra, examining an upside-down bike on the side of the main road, the bike's chain hanging slack. An illicit bench picnic, spread out between two women who popped the cork from a bottle of prosecco and poured it into plastic flutes. It was all very different to the city, where the rules were tightly observed: you could leave your house once a day, and only once a day, for a singular, socially distanced walk, or to buy groceries, that was all. A sense of furtiveness and urgency hung over people back in Bristol, but I sensed none of that down here. It was a slower, calmer existence, and simple acts like being outside felt more inconsequential. People acting in the spirit of the law, rather than to the letter. I liked it. It made me feel like there was space to breathe, which was something I had not had in the city for some long time.

One thing remained the same, though, regrettably: the seagulls. There were seagulls everywhere, just like Bristol, sitting on roofs, shitting on people, wheeling above the bay, decorating boats with thick globs of pasty white guano, squabbling over leftover fish suppers lying on the road in their wrappers—thank god the takeaways and fish and chip shops were still open—squawking and screeching endlessly. I wasn't keen on the gulls, I found their penetrating eyes unappealing, not to mention their harsh, mournful screeches, but I could tolerate sea birds more than I could tolerate urban birds, especially the ragged, scruffy pigeons that hobbled and flapped about in large, tatty clouds back home.

Not long after lunchtime, we found ourselves driving along the seafront of one particularly small, quaint fishing village called Mousehole. I had to edge along the narrow street slowly, for both pedestrians and gulls alike had little reason to care about traffic, and I frequently found myself hammering the brakes as someone wandered out in front of me without looking. Here, residents had the natural advantage over cars, for the streets were so slender it was impossible to build up any speed beyond a crawl.

"What are all these people doing outside?" Dad murmured, echoing my sentiments as we nudged along. "I thought we were all supposed to be in lockdown."

I thought about making a comment, something to do with how Dad, more than anyone, should understand that people can't be locked inside without going mad, but I refrained.

"This is the last town before the estate," I said instead, turning right and changing gear clumsily to accommodate a steep, sharply ascending street that could only ever fit one vehicle on it at a time. Dad nodded.

"It's got that feel to it," he said, although I had no idea what that meant. A final frontier, perhaps? It was a touch dramatic for him as far as imagery went.

"It's a four-mile walk if you need anything. There's a coastal path that starts up here on the left, I think. You can follow the cliffs all the way along until you get to our place."

"That's nice. There wasn't a lot of opportunity to walk in prison."

"My thoughts exactly. It will be good for us. We could both use a little—*fuck!*"

I screeched to a halt as a small white van careened around a sharp corner and downhill, meeting me head on, refusing to back up. I waved a hand at the bald-headed driver behind the wheel: it was a lot easier for him to reverse than me, and he knew it.

"Your mother used to do that, you know," Dad murmured as the van sat stubbornly in the road. "She was bullish, in the car. She would never give way."

I was not my mother, and so reluctantly, when it became obvious that the driver of the van was not going to do anything to help me out, I caved, reversing down the street until I reached a small junction, which gave just enough space for the van to squeeze past and turn down a side road. I glared out of my window as he did so, thinking sourly that drivers were no better in the country than in the city. The man, who looked to be about Dad's age, smirked as he passed, reveling in the fact that he'd won.

He lifted his two index fingers on the steering wheel

to acknowledge the sacrifice I had made as he went by. The gesture brought to mind a pair of cow's horns, on either side of the leather steering wheel's head.

Dad made a funny noise in his throat. I glanced over and caught him staring at the driver's hands.

"What's up?" I thought I could see recognition on Dad's face, which was a shade paler than it had been a moment ago.

"Nothing. It's just..." He replicated the two-index-finger gesture, making cow's horns of his own. "Just like your mother used to do," Dad said quietly.

"Enough of that, please," I replied, feeling a little unnerved, because he was right. The gesture was identical to how my mum would acknowledge other drivers: two index fingers high, horns pointing front. But so what? People made familiar gestures every day, there were only so many things you could do with your hands when they were holding the steering wheel. I found I was annoyed with myself for how I was reacting. I took it out on Dad, snapping at him in an unnecessarily hard tone of voice.

"I don't have the bandwidth to go down memory lane right now, if that's okay. Stop looking for things to get upset about."

"Sorry," Dad mumbled, and we fell into an uneasy silence.

I started back up the hill again, sighing. I was more

tired than I'd been willing to admit to when we left the
city, left our house. The weight of what we were doing
was beginning to press upon me. Unfamiliar surroundings, no matter how welcomed and anticipated, were
still unfamiliar, still taxing. I chugged into a lower gear
and put my foot down, pushing faster up the hill this
time, determined to get to the top of it unchallenged.
One showdown a day was plenty enough for my nerves.

"Some nice pubs here," Dad remarked after we'd
breached the hill and carried on through the outskirts of
the tiny town. "Maybe we could get Sunday lunch once
or twice. When things open up again. They can't stay
closed forever."

"I'd like that," I said, wanting to smooth over my
bad temper, but I didn't think, secretly, that they'd be
open for a long time, and when they did, I was doubtful
we would be able to afford it. These were tourist towns
in the summer, and the prices reflected that, I was sure. I
hadn't told Dad yet that I was broke. There was no
reason to tell him, to make him feel even more guilt.
That kind of information was on a strictly need-to-know
basis.

The car churned through another gear change as we
left the town behind us and climbed up a huge bone of
granite, where the road levelled out, following the coastline closely, hugging its curves and inlets, and it was as if
the whole Atlantic Ocean—or was it the Celtic Sea? I

never was too good at geography—was suddenly laid out next to us like a brilliant green-blue blanket, for the fog lifted momentarily and an unexpected bolt of sun seized its moment, leapt through, highlighting a particular narrow curved spit of rock that thrust out into the sea like a coat hook up ahead. Upon it, we could make out a dark, tall, man-made shape that punctuated the horizon like an exclamation mark.

"What's that?" Dad asked, shading his eyes. He was not used to such bright sun. "A lighthouse?"

"Not quite." I found a small layby and pulled into it, switching off and letting the car engine cool down a little.

"Then what?"

"That," I said, pulling out my phone and texting my contact that we were ten minutes away, "is the Folly."

"The Folly?"

I hit send, pocketed my phone, took in a deep, full breath of sea air. I wanted the salt to wash my lungs clean of the city smog, but I knew that would take time.

"Our new home, Dad," I said, and the beam of sun disappeared as if shut off at the source, but that was okay. I knew the Folly was still down there, waiting. A home did not always need to be bathed in sun to be a good place to live.

SEVEN

"The job is simple. Keep everything running, keep it in good working order. Check the grounds twice a day, check the fences are sound and able to keep trespassers out, be visible, discourage vandalism. It is quiet around here, for obvious reasons, but we still have issues with the local teenagers sometimes. And the death tourists, obviously."

"Death tourists?"

The owner waved Dad's question away, intent on getting through his instructions.

"The young'uns like to light fires in the woods at the edge of the estate, drink, do drugs, that sort of nonsense. Not serious enough to involve the police, but not exactly desirable either."

He had met us at the small gravel parking spot at the end of the road, as instructed. It wasn't possible to drive right up to the Folly, as the architect had designed the place before roads were a consideration, so a small field at the end of the lane had been set aside for visitors and estate folk to park in. Some distance from it, the Folly top loomed above a low line of hedgerow, as if frowning upon us.

A decorative, brooding, and yet wholly frivolous endeavour, the Folly was a tall black granite tower with distinct crenellations capping the roof. It sat stoically on the very tip of a craggy, hooked peninsula, rising confidently above the sea as if it belonged to another era, as if ancient kings had resided there once. It reminded me of the novels of Tolkien and C.S. Lewis: an evocative, dark column that seemed almost otherworldly when the light caught the blue sea behind it in just the right way.

The Folly had once been part of the estate of an earl, built in the Georgian era several miles from the main house, as a bolt hole for the man of the estate to escape to as necessary. For a while, the owner explained as he passed over a heavy iron key and then a series of smaller keys, it had been used only to store hunting equipment, but as the years passed, it took on some notoriety, for two reasons. The first, that a local author had written a novel about the tower, a hugely successful romance thriller in the style of Fowles called *The Wailing Pillar*, where the protagonist, a woman who bore a remarkable resemblance to the author herself, had tragically leapt from the rooftop and into the sea below the cliffs at the climax. Looking at the Folly, I could see that, logistically, it wasn't possible to land in the ocean by jumping from the tower, not unless you flew a few hundred feet first, but I assumed novelists didn't mind about logistics if it came at the expense of a good story. There had been a movie based on the book in the seventies, and tourism in the area still relied heavily on that. Go into any local pub, the owner said, and you would find faded glossy photos of the cast in full period costume, wigs and all, grinning over pints of Cornish IPA and plates of battered fish.

The second reason, and one I tried not to think about too deeply as I slept my first night in the Folly, was that the aforementioned author of the novel, a much-liked local called Jessica Harbourne, had, upon growing increasingly obsessed with the structure and the imaginary world she had built for herself within, broken into the empty building late one night, two days after her divorce had finalised, and offered herself to gravity in the exact same manner that the heroine of her book had done, without ceremony. She had not landed in the sea, for obvious reasons. She had landed on the green, shortly cropped grass below, and that, as the saying goes, had been that.

After, the Folly became a pilgrimage site for tourists —what the owner called death tourists—and fans of both book and movie. He had caught several other young, sad, impressionable women attempting to break into the tower in the dead of the night for what he could only assume were similar reasons, he said.

That was why he needed us to watch the place.

"It's funny," he mused, scratching his chin and shaking his head as we watched rabbits peacefully hopping around on the scrubby grass at the base of the tower. "How communicable tragedy is, isn't it? It's like a disease, sadness. One person can pass it along to another so easily. Like a bloody virus."

I didn't particularly want to dwell on this sort of thing, not in front of Dad (I didn't want him putting any ideas into my father's head), but I let the man talk, because it was clear he hadn't spoken to many other people for a while. None of us had, really, thanks to the state of the world, although I had to remind myself not to say that out loud around Dad, who had suffered an isolation far worse than any of us could imagine. I was also in no position to interrupt the person who was ostensibly paying our rent and food bills for the foreseeable future, so Dad and I both leaned back on our heels in that slow, heavy way we had and let the owner have his moment.

"So you can see why we need someone in there

around the clock," he continued, putting his hands in his large wax jacket pockets. "We used to let the place out as a holiday home, and that did well enough for a while, but with this bloody pandemic...well, nobody is going on holiday anymore, are they? I've already had to chase one lot of squatters out of here. The type that think ownership is nine-tenths of the law. Do you know they tried to tell me that after a certain number of weeks, I can't move them along? Citing bloody adverse possession laws at me. I was having none of it. Looked into it; they'd have needed to be living here for ten years before they could even think about claiming any type of ownership! They made a hell of a mess with graffiti on their way out. Smoked out the entire place with the wrong type of wood in the fireplace, too, and you don't want to know what condition they left the toilet in. I suppose possession really is nine-tenths of the law, eh? That's why I need you two."

Dad and I exchanged glances and I smiled as sympathetically as I could. It felt like a hollow gesture. It was always difficult with rich folk, feeling sympathy, and besides, I was itching to get inside and check out the place. I was tired after our long drive, and needed to put my feet up.

The owner sensed my impatience.

"Yes, well. Let's go in, shall we?"

We followed him across the expanse of green littered

with rabbit droppings and small, half-dug burrows that could have been homes for seabirds or rodents, I couldn't tell which.

"Watch your ankles here," the owner said without looking back. "Damn rabbits leave bloody holes everywhere."

He showed me how to use the large key in the only door at ground level. It had a substantial cast iron lock on it that was from another era, and required a certain technique to engage the key fully, owing to how heavy it was and how lopsided the lock had become over time. A quick, sharp thrust in, an even sharper twist to the right, then to the left to loosen the mechanisms, and then to the right again, this time all the way around. It felt like a ceremony, a welcome ritual.

Inside, a series of round rooms were arranged on top of each other like stacking cups. A ground-floor boot room faced us as we went in through the door, tiled with huge stone flagstones. From here, the cast iron staircase that wound all the way to the top of the Folly started, spiraling up through each room. Each fan-shaped step was fashioned from ornate metal painted a glossy black, and was narrower at one end than the other, to accommodate for the twists of each spiral. The whole thing was style over substance, an unnecessarily elaborate, impractical, and, to my eyes, dangerous device.

Dad and I exchanged looks when we first saw the

staircase, both of us probably thinking the same thought.

Would be really easy to fall down that, wouldn't it?

The owner chattered on while we tried to get our bearings.

"There's space for coats, boots, wet gear—you'll have a lot, living here—and your firewood store is tucked off there in that bunker," the owner said, levering off his wellington boots and starting up the steps. "Boiler's on the wall there; it's just been serviced so you shouldn't have any problems for a bit."

We also shed our shoes and followed him. The steps made loud rattling noises beneath our careful feet. I gripped onto the cold, thin metal stair rail tightly, thinking about Mum, and trying not to.

What are you going to do? I scolded myself as we ascended slowly. *Live in houses without stairs for the rest of your life?*

The living room was next. Perfectly round, it was sparsely decorated and could only accommodate single armchairs rather than a full-sized couch, but I was alright with that. I didn't see myself snuggling up to Dad whilst watching TV, not yet. A bit of space between us wouldn't hurt. Besides, looking at the television set, I was doubtful how functional it was. Perhaps we'd be playing a lot of cards instead.

The living room was carpeted with a thick pile rug,

and there were pictures on the walls, all nautical in nature: etchings of ships cresting the waves of a stormy sea, sails pregnant with violent wind, ships docked in harbour, ships out on placid waters, palm trees and bright sunshine accessorising various tropical scenes. It was all very Treasure Island, and the pictures suited the building, which sported round porthole style windows that showcased deep turquoise on one side of the tower, and rolling countryside on the other. A fireplace formed the centrepiece of the room, with a small copper-rimmed hearth loaded with a wood basket, a poker, and tongs jutting out. "Try not to trip on the edges of that, it's a bugger for the ankles," the owner said, and I resolved to get some tape, mark off the hearth as a hazard so that Dad could better navigate it. He'd gotten clumsy while inside, and with doctors being so hard to get hold of in the current circumstances, I didn't want to take any risks.

I could see a patch of well-scrubbed wall near the sea-facing window, and remembered what the owner said about squatters leaving graffiti. I wondered what it had been of, whether it was sprayed art or territorial tagging. Either way, the clean-up attempt looked uglier than what had probably been scoured away, and I tried and failed not to think about the house I'd left behind, of rubbing Mum's blood off the walls. I was always trying not to think about that. I wished with all my heart that I could scrub the persistent memory from my mind the way I scrubbed Mum's brains off the bottom step of my old family home, but I knew it would be a long, long time before I was able to forget that day, forget being that person, forget sobbing and retching and then numbly watching the brain-water flush away down the toilet. After, I had climbed into a shower turned so hot it had nearly peeled the skin clean off my bones, and I had lowered myself to the floor and sat there whilst the water fell on top of my head and down my shoulders and back, and I had cried so hard I had felt something break inside me, like a twig audibly snapping in two, and after that I had driven to the hardware store and bought three tins of buttercup yellow paint and gone to town with it.

But that was in the past and this was in the now, and I had to remind myself of that, forcibly.

The next level was a small kitchenette, equipped with a tiny AGA stove upon which an old-fashioned whistling kettle sat, and not much else aside from some alcove shelving, a fridge, and a toaster. Worktop space was minimal, but that was okay. It was only the two of us: I was hardly going to be turning out five-course banquets any time soon.

Above the kitchen, a bathroom, with a tiny sit-up style copper bath straight out of the eighteen hundreds resting on another deep-pile rug, only this tub was plumbed in, with a giant pair of chrome taps connected to a huge copper pipe that fed down to the boiler on the ground floor. There was a small porcelain sink, no bigger than a dinner plate, mounted on one wall with a mirror hanging over, and a squat toilet with a cistern tank high up above it, operated by a pull chain.

The spartan nature of the Folly was something of a relief. It would be easy to keep clean, by necessity: there was no space for clutter or mess. That had been the biggest challenge in our old house. Mum had kept it regimentally clean, but she had also been fond of collecting trinkets, knick-knacks, ornaments, and it had all required constant dusting, sorting, reorganising, and I often thought Mum liked to make work for herself in that way—she had needed things to do, to be occupied and useful.

I was looking forward to a simpler way of life.

Above the bathroom, sat two bedrooms, or rather, one bedroom with a tiny attic space above, the ceiling of which formed the very top of the tower. Dad expressed an interest in the attic room because it had larger windows than the rooms on the lower levels. I granted the request without argument. Prison had restricted his access to daylight. I wasn't about to do the same. If he wanted to look at the sea and the sky, I was happy for him to do so. Perhaps it would bring him some peace.

The tour of the Folly complete, we all traipsed back

down the steps carefully until we were at the ground floor level again, in the boot room. The owner slipped his wellies back on, and asked us what we thought.

"I like it," I said, and I meant it. The Folly was quiet, remote, beautifully situated and looked to be easy to keep clean and take care of. It was the perfect place for a middle-aged, childless woman and her father to set up anew.

Dad kept quiet. He would tell me what he thought at some point, once he had figured it out. This could take some time, I knew. He never was very good at identifying his own feelings. Mum had always done that for him. Through her, he had known himself better, I realised, and without her, he was facing an identity crisis larger than I'd considered possible while he was in prison when someone was on hand every hour of every day to tell him what he could and couldn't do.

"You'll be quite comfortable here," the owner said, sensing Dad's unease.

"I'm sure we will," Dad replied, non-committal.

The owner did not seem offended. I remembered he had experience with people like Dad, people with a past that was difficult to translate into a future, and I felt immensely and suddenly grateful to the man for giving us the opportunity he was extending. I said as much, stopping short of giving him an awkward hug.

He waved me off affably. "A couple of things left to

say," he continued, all business and no fuss, which I appreciated. "One, you don't have to worry about heading into town for food or groceries if you don't want to. Nobody's supposed to leave their house unless it's for essentials anyway at the moment, although hardly anyone around here is following that guidance. I'm sure you noticed as you drove through town." He snorted, waving in the direction of Mousehole, and we echoed him with our own snorts of derisive agreement.

"Anyway, I've organised a delivery to come to the end of the lane once a week, on Tuesdays. All paid for, just text and let me know if you want any of the items on the list changing. You'll have to fetch them yourself —the driver can't get the van up any closer, and anyway, he is not insured to bring the goods over the fence and across to the Folly itself. But I'm sure you'll manage."

I nodded and made the appropriate noises to show I was still paying attention, although I was so tired, I was finding it hard to focus.

"Same for firewood. You should have enough in the wood store to cover you until the autumn. During the summer it does get a little chilly at night, what with the wind and how exposed the place is, but you'll have enough to see you through. Don't be tempted to forage for wood if you run low, please. You have to use the right sort of wood, like I said, or the chimney will catch fire, and we don't want that. It's a listed building, for one thing, and also very expensive to get a fire crew out here, trust me. Especially in the middle of a bloody pandemic. So if you do run out of wood, text, let me know, and I'll get a delivery to you. Don't burn anything else in the fireplace. Please."

"Understood," I said solemnly.

"Third, the weather down here can change at the drop of a hat, so get used to how changeable it is. There is a weather station on the top of the tower, linked to a small notification board in the kitchen. Brand new, digital. It'll give you alerts when things are particularly bad. If the wind speed gets up above thirty-five knots, start exercising caution outside. It has been known for people to get swept off the peninsula by unexpected gusts. We had nearly eighty knots a week or so back."

"Oh?" My blank expression betrayed my ignorance while my mind galloped off into a dozen wet and windy scenarios, all of them involving Dad, so frail and light-weight, being yanked off the cliff-edge and out to sea.

"That's over ninety miles per hour." The owner helpfully applied context to his speak of knots.

"Oh."

"A person doesn't do well wandering along a narrow cliff peninsula when the wind is at those speeds."

"Noted," I said, feeling my anxiety creep up another few notches.

"Other than that, it should all be self-explanatory,"

the owner concluded, moving on as if people getting knocked off the edge of the country and into the ocean never to be seen again was no big deal. "My landline number, should you lose it, is on a note pinned to this board over here, along with other useful numbers if you get into any trouble. But you won't. It's all quite straightforward. I daresay you'll find it a little boring, even. Just keep an eye on the place, look out for trouble, keep it safe from any nonsense. And watch out for those pesky death tourists, they can be a real nuisance."

The owner checked his watch then. "Your first grocery delivery is due in half an hour, so I'll let you get on. Just the basics, but it should see you through the week. Call me if you need anything else. Oh, and I should have said, mobile phone signal is spotty out here at best. You stand a better chance higher up the tower if you need anything urgent."

"Right," I said, nodding.

"Good exercise if nothing else, hey?" He laughed, and I forced myself to join in.

"On that note, one more thing," the owner said, remembering a last piece of information. "It also goes without saying, walking around these parts is very beautiful. Good for the soul, eh? The coastal path goes right past this place and all the way along, for miles, but don't get too close to the cliff edges. I know I sound like a terrible bore, but they can crumble and give way without warning, especially after all the bad weather we've had recently. Just be careful, eh?"

Dad spoke up then. It was the first time he had opened his mouth in a while.

"Long way down, is it?"

The owner chuckled. "If the tide was in, you might stand a chance, but even then, the rocks go deep and sharp under the water, so I wouldn't recommend you take up diving any time soon."

"Pity," Dad said. "I was looking for a new hobby." I recognised that he was trying his first real attempt at humour since he had left prison. This was a good sign, even if the subject matter was a little on the dark side.

We're going to be alright, I thought, a small hope flowering in my chest.

The sun broke free from the clouds once more, throwing the Folly into high relief as the owner took his leave at last. I didn't usually believe in signs, but this was as good a time to start as any, I supposed.

EIGHT

On the first night, I heard Dad moving around in his room above me, out of bed, restless. It was very late, and I was just drifting into a deep, exhausted sleep when a series of thumps and grunts and a loud muffled bang rang out into the quiet. Thinking the worst, without knowing really what that was, I bolted out of bed and scrambled up the narrow iron stairs that led through my bedroom ceiling towards Dad's room. There was only just enough space to get comfortably up the stairwell, which was proving to be a true cold spot in the Folly, channeling damp, chilly air freely up and down the structure no matter what the temperature was outside.

Because the top of the staircase represented the top of the building, it stopped abruptly at a little platform outside the attic room that was closed off from the rest of the tower by a sturdy door, instead of the open shaft holes that featured in the rooms below. I suspected the privacy this afforded had also been a reason Dad wanted the top room, but now I questioned my intelligence in allowing him that privacy.

"Dad?" I said, rapping on his door sharply. "What are you doing in there?"

It took him a moment or two to open up, and I wondered if I was overstepping a boundary, but I had to be sure he wasn't doing anything dangerous to himself. I had read the statistics about prisoners after release. The details were grim. I had fought hard to get him back. I wasn't about to lose him now, not after everything we'd been through.

When his face appeared, alongside a blast of cold, salty air, it looked guilty, but resigned. I was immensely relieved to see him. I don't know what I had expected exactly, but I was just happy he was still there. Relief gave way quickly to my own guilt. Randomised night-time searches of prisoner's cells had been a regular thing where Dad had been incarcerated. It kept the inmates tired, unsure of themselves, and without any true sense of privacy or agency over their own space. I had to remind myself that interruptions like these were invasive and not good for his state of mind, no matter how worthwhile I considered the reason. I needed to wash the stink of prison off Dad once and for all. That meant stability. I needed to be less anxious.

I softened my tone, and my posture. "What are you doing in there, Dad? You woke me up."

"Sorry, love," he mumbled, and stood obediently aside to show me a trapdoor in the bedroom ceiling, which I'd somehow not noticed before. He'd gotten it open, and pulled down another folding step ladder attached to the other side of the door. "Turns out I can't sleep on soft beds, not yet. Thought I'd do a spot of stargazing instead."

I could see glimmering pricks of light through the open trapdoor, which led to a small stone platform at the top of the Folly. I wondered instantly whether this was the platform from where the infamous author lady had hurled herself years before.

"You should be sleeping, Dad. So should I."

He ignored that. "Remember when you were little and we'd stargaze in the back garden?"

I nodded. Of course I did. I remembered most things about my childhood in vivid detail. It had been a happy one, full of bright, colourful moments. Those moments had helped me when Mum had died, because I knew I would always have them. The right memories were gifts, and all I needed was to stay inside them, to dwell in the sunshine and picnics and day trips and pretty dresses and castles and farms and holidays instead of remembering that time I had scraped my own mother's brain matter that had dried hard and crusty into the weave of the hall rug off first with my fingernails and then with her toothbrush—she wouldn't be needing it anymore—when nothing else would work to lift it from the oriental weft.

We climbed unsteadily up onto the roof, where a couple of rusty bistro chairs had been folded and stacked to one side against the tower's stone lip. We set them up, sitting down gingerly in case they broke and collapsed, and found we had a good view of the Milky Way. It was a clear night, the clearest I'd seen for a long, long time. I reveled in the countryside atmosphere as I settled back in my seat. In the city, the stars were never as bright, the sky never as dark, the air never as pure. From my cold perch, I could hear the sea battering the cliffs far down below, and a sliver of moon reflected on the ocean miles out toward the horizon. It was a peaceful, restorative moment. I hoped Dad was enjoying it as much as I was.

I looked over and tried to read his face in the starlight. His profile was picked out with a distinct shining outline, as if he were an art deco print.

"Your mother named you for the sea, you know," he said. "It's a Welsh name."

"I know."

"I miss her."

"I miss her, too."

He let out a deep, long breath. "You can ask me about it, if you like. That night. With your Mum. We never really spoke about it, not in person, what with—"

I held up a hand to ward off his words.

"It's okay."

"Morgan..."

I sighed. There was always something. Always. Never a peaceful moment that one could enjoy at leisure. Only snatched micro-moments, borrowed and never owned.

I sharpened my tone. It made me feel once again as if I were the parent, not the child, but then it had been that way since the night Dad had been taken into custody.

"I don't want to talk about it. It's in the past now." I tried to be as firm as possible, but Dad was emboldened by the night, by the stars he had not seen for many years.

"I thought you'd have questions," he said. His eyes were shadowy hollows in his face.

I looked at the moon and swallowed down a hard lump in my throat. "What good are questions, or answers, for that matter? She's still dead. It won't change anything."

He thought about it. "I suppose that's true."

"Remember when you showed me how to find the Plough?" I pointed to it, tracing the path between seven stars with my index finger.

"I remember." He squinted, traced the line, too. It felt like sign language, a particular type reserved just for us. It always had.

"Dad," I said after a long pause. "We're going to be okay, you know." It sounded more like a question than a statement, for I was very unsure of myself in that moment.

But my father was no longer listening to me. His attention was focused on a small bright spot of light that danced and waggled around on the edge of the peninsula below.

I leaned forward in my chair, spotting it too. We both watched it for a while.

"What's that?" I murmured.

"Torch light," Dad replied quietly.

"Someone prowling?"

"Looks like."

"Death tourist?"

"Or maybe just someone walking the dog."

"We'll be able to tell if that light takes a sudden tumble off the cliff."

"Morgan, don't talk like that." Dad tsked, but I could tell he was amused despite himself.

We kept watch. The light bobbed up and down, matching the motion of someone walking slowly.

"They're getting closer," Dad observed. There was a territorial edge to his voice.

The bobbing pinprick of light grew larger. Soon we could make out the dark silhouette of a figure walking with measured intent towards the tower. There was no stopping and starting, no hesitancy that betrayed a lack of sense of direction or knowledge of the landscape. If anything, the light seemed to know exactly where it was going, which unnerved me a little. Was this how it was going to be every night? Watching for night prowlers from the top of the Folly like Roman sentinels guarding Hadrian's wall?

The light stopped at the foot of the Folly, stabilised for a moment. I had a sense of someone standing below us, looking up.

Dad shouted down in his most intimidating voice.

"Hey! This is private property! Clear off before I call the police!"

Silence answered him. The light did not waver.

Had they even heard? Could they see us, perched on the roof, peering down through the crenellations? It seemed impossible that they could, through the darkness. And yet.

The light remained.

"I said clear off! Go on now!" Dad still had some mettle in him, and I felt a sudden rush of relief for how authoritative he had become. How protective.

"I mean it!"

The light hovered in place a little longer, as if in defiance, before slowly moving along again, gradually getting smaller, and then finally disappearing off into the night.

"Odd," I said, when I was sure it had gone, sighing heavily and sitting back in my chair.

Dad said nothing. He remained on high alert, watching the world below us like a guard dog, ears pricked, prepared for more trespassers.

We went to bed several hours later, cold, exhausted, as dawn's light began to stain the horizon behind us. Dad, despite his protestations that he wouldn't be able to, slumbered heavily. I heard him snoring through my ceiling, a domineering, rhythmic buzz that penetrated every part of my brain.

He slept. I didn't.

NINE

The morning, when I woke up, was drenched in sunshine. Clear skies leeched into the still, flat ocean, and the world around me popped with vivid hues: green and blue, green and blue. I took my first coffee of the day outside on a small wooden bench placed at the foot of the Folly. Wrapped only in a thin sleep shirt and long dressing gown, I let the cool sea breeze snake around my shivering limbs and breathed deep of the salty air as I gripped my scalding hot cup tightly in both hands. I felt a good deal more alive than I had in a very, very long time, despite my lack of sleep. Sleep would come, I reasoned. I was simply adjusting to a new way of life. It would take time. I had to be as patient with myself as I was with Dad.

I stared at the ocean for some time, hypnotised by

the enormity of it, until I saw, eventually, a small black blob slice through the waves some distance out. Thinking at first that it was my eyes playing tricks, I fetched a pair of binoculars from their peg by the Folly's front door. A colourful chart had been pinned next to them: marine life commonly sighted in the area. I studied it for a second, then went back to the bench, balancing my coffee carefully on the bench slats beside me, scanning the sea for the blob with the binoculars. After what felt like an eternity of futile searching, I found it again. It was a fin, moving fast and streamlined, like an obsidian knife slicing through wet blue butter. Dolphin? I couldn't tell. Still, it felt good to see. Thrilling, almost. I liked thinking about creatures swimming around down there in the depths, submarine beasts going about their business: hunting, eating, mating. It felt reassuring, somehow, a reminder that life carried on regardless, no matter what personal dramas and tragedies played out up here, for the ocean was always a constant, and so was the sky. We were simple inhabitants, a tiny part of a vast microcosm of moving parts. It was comforting to think about, because it reminded me I had a place in the overall scheme of things, and it had been hard to feel like that after Mum died. I had been displaced for a long time. But here, sitting in my dressing gown with cold dew kissing my bare feet, bracketed by blue sky and bluer sea, I felt as if I belonged.

Perhaps it was because Mum had always loved the sea, too. I felt closer to her in that moment than I had for a long time. Like I could finally start to push the trauma of her grisly death to one side and be closer to the real version of her.

I swept the binoculars around to take in the rest of the horizon, and then eventually, as I scanned along, the tip of the peninsula upon which the Folly stood. It would take time getting used to the lack of urban land-scape. My eyes, through the round lenses, were filled with water, stone, grass, rabbits, sky, birds swooping and wheeling, more sea, more grass, and—

I felt my heart lurch as something unexpected came into view.

At first it was a mere fuzzy blob interrupting the coastal scenery, a familiar upright shape that was out of focus until I instinctively adjusted the focal ring, and found...

It was the figure of a man, bald-headed, who was turned toward me. His face filled my vision, too large, so all I could see was his pale skin, his huge eyes. Startled, I kept twisting the focal ring around until I found a clear, circular portrait of him at the end of my binoculars, and saw that he was smiling.

Spooked, I dropped the heavy instrument into my lap, swearing and spilling my coffee—which had been balanced next to me, against my thigh—down my legs, burning myself. Yelping in pain, I frantically wiped at my bare, stinging skin as red welts raised up almost immediately on my calves. I looked up again, squinting into the low morning sun, trying to locate the source of my discomfort, only to find the man who had been standing on the end of the peninsula as bold as brass (as if he had been there all along, when I knew for sure he hadn't) strolling determinedly toward me.

Was this the same person who had been wandering around in the dark late last night?

Something about the speed at which he walked made me suddenly very uncomfortable. What did he want? I was in no mood to talk to strangers, it was too early and I was barely dressed.

My heart thumped fast.

Where was Dad?

I half-rose from my seat, hoping to dart inside before the stranger reached me, but my coffee-splattered dressing gown snagged on one end of a loose slat of the wooden bench. I fumbled with it, swearing, all my fingers turned to thumbs, clumsy in my haste. I did not want to take the gown off just to avoid saying hello—I was not wearing any underwear under my sleep shirt, and the cool wind would make that abundantly apparent within moments of taking off the wrapper garment.

I yanked at the fabric as the man came closer, but it was stuck fast.

"Dad!" I called, suddenly panicking without really knowing why. "*Dad!*"

Then I realised what an idiot I was being.

I had nothing to be afraid of. This was just a man taking a walk. On private property, sure, but people did that sort of thing all the time in the countryside. I had to learn to relax, stop taking everything so seriously.

Nothing bad was happening, and nothing bad was about to happen. Thoughts were not facts, after all.

Get a hold of yourself, I self-admonished.

I only just about managed to calm myself by the time the man, whose head shone like polished stone in the sunlight, arrived at my bench.

"This is private land," I said, breathless and embarrassed and not a little unsettled. I huddled into my dressing gown, hoping against hope I was adequately covered up in all the essential places.

The man loomed over me, extremely tall and intimidating. He looked strong, solid, like he worked a hard manual job. He also looked familiar, but I couldn't place why.

"It is?" he replied, and his voice was immediately off-putting in that it was oddly high-pitched. It also reminded me of someone, but I was having a hard time thinking straight and couldn't bring who immediately to mind.

At that moment, Dad, who had heard me calling, came out of the Folly's front door.

"Alright, love?" he said, marching over to stand protectively next to me and face the stranger.

When Dad got a good look at the man's face, however, I felt him go rigid.

"Hello, Owen," the stranger replied in that soft, high tone, and for an awful, awful moment, I thought he was speaking...I thought...

I knew it was impossible, but...

The man spoke with Mum's voice.

Dad went pale. He stared. Eventually, he managed to recover enough to croak out a challenge.

"Who are you?"

"Don't you recognise me, darling?" The stranger said.

Dad went even stiffer. His posture was now so brittle I thought he might shatter if the breeze hit him the wrong way.

"I have never seen you before in my life," he replied, coldly.

I was sure this was a lie as soon as the words fell from his lips.

"Now clear off out of here. It's private land."

The stranger smiled again, more of a smirk this time, and I hated it.

Then he did something that made my blood freeze.

He lifted one hand to the side of his head, several inches from his temple, and began to twirl his index finger around in the air, over and over again.

At first, I thought he was making the "crazy person" motion with his finger, but the circular action was too broad and erratic for that. Then, as the creeping pull of recognition coaxed goosebumps up on my flesh, I understood what he was actually doing. I understood, and thought I would drown in the wave of icy revulsion that swept over me.

For he was not making a motion or indication of any sort.

No, rather, he was twirling an imaginary strand of long hair through his fingers, round and round and through and round again, just like...

Just like...

In exactly the same way Mum used to do when she was alive.

Watching television.

On the phone.

Reading a book.

A distracted, obsessive motion.

Twiddle, twirl, twiddle, twirl...

My own hand went up to the close-cropped hair on my head.

Dad made a funny noise deep in the base of his throat.

The man smiled fondly at us both, still circling the air with his finger.

Twirl, twiddle, twirl...

I looked down at my coffee-stained lap, unable to watch anymore. The welts on my legs were already bright scarlet, and they burned enough to bring tears to my eyes.

"Owen?" the man said again in that awful, false voice. "Aren't you going to kiss me hello?"

Dad grabbed me by the arm and yanked at my trapped dressing gown, ripping it clean in two in his efforts to free it from the grip of the bench, before bundling us both back into the Folly through the narrow single door, locking and bolting it firmly behind us. I didn't much care about the gown anymore, and didn't offer any protest. I just wanted to get away from the stranger, I wanted to get away from him more than I knew how to express.

"Dad?" I asked, shaken by the weird encounter and looking for reassurance. "Who was that? Do you know him?"

Dad shook his head, but wouldn't meet my eyes. "Just some nut," he replied.

Through a small peephole in the door, we watched as the man continued to twirl his non-existent hair in one hand, head cocked inquisitively to the side, staring directly as if he could still see us through the thick wooden door, which, of course, he couldn't.

But it sure felt like he could.

Eventually, he shook himself, like a dog shaking water from his fur. A queer expression crossed his face. He looked as if he was waking up from a deep sleep. He then started, and spun around as if surprised to find himself standing where he was. Shaking his head violently, muttering to himself, he stumbled off in the direction of the field where our car was parked, and I did not see him after that, not for the rest of the day, at least.

Half an hour later, the sky clouded over, and the rain began.

I could hardly hear it through the daze of my memories.

Mum, twirling her hair absentmindedly through her fingers.

Mum, lying broken at the foot of the stairs.

Did she fall or was she pushed? the papers had asked, all bold red lettering. For a while, it had seemed as if that question was on every website, every social media post, everywhere I looked. Someone even spray-painted it on a wall near our house in Bristol. I hated that her life had been reduced to such a question, because she had been greater than that, she had been greater than the sum of her demise, but getting anyone to understand had been an impossible endeavour, so I'd given up trying to convince people this was not how she should be remembered and instead, I'd internalised our past together until I'd almost forgotten it. The public discourse had rendered our time on earth as mother and daughter an almost shameful occurrence, and that was something I would never be able to forgive. Ever.

This was a large part of why I wanted to retreat from the world, from the public in general. From the meanness, the discourse, the lack of nuance, the lack of compassion. It was all too much. Too simplified, and yet too complicated in the same breath.

Out here, I should have felt better able to connect with my past.

For the memories were still there, buried beneath layers of denial and self-preservation and emotional restraint, memories of fresh bread baking, of photograph albums meticulously labelled, of fastidious neatness, of bleach and ornaments and the way she answered the phone even when she knew it was me: "Yes? Hello? Who's that?"

Her fingers, working on those longer strands of thick, shiny hair.

That particular memory was tainted now. It morphed and merged with the image of a middle-aged man, tall, broad-shouldered, bald, hard of face and feature, his hand in the air, poised in an affected manner, twirling sweet nothing around and around and around his index finger, an idiot smile on his lips.

TEN

Later that day, a howling storm hit.

Strangely exhausted from my early morning encounter, I had fallen into a fitful sleep on my chair in the living room. As clouds gathered outside, I dreamt about the strange man and Mum dancing together on the narrow hook-end of the peninsula, sea spray exploding like white, frothy lava from below, framing a macabre waltz that seemed more like a struggle for dominance than a musical ritual or celebration of intimacy, that felt more like fighting or wrestling than dancing, and just as a colossal peal of thunder woke me up, Mum and the stranger struggled themselves right off the edge of the cliffs, and one could only assume they ended up on the rocks below, shattered and broken, yet still locked in step, and for a moment, as I clambered up the slippery slope of wakefulness, all I could see was Mum's blood, and I hoped this was not a permanent regression, for it had taken me nearly seven years to shake the red from my sight every time I closed my eyes.

Dragged into semi-awareness by the thunderclap, I found I had tears on my cheeks. I dabbed at them with my sleeve. I did not feel rested in the slightest.

Thunder pealed overhead again. I jolted fully awake, and looked about, disoriented. The living room was now as gloomy and shadowed as the sky outside, and felt crowded, close and dark. Rain hammered the glass port-hole windows. It sounded like gravel being flung at the panes with tremendous force. I hoped they were strong enough to withstand the assault.

Mum's picture from our old kitchen hung nearby. Her face looked down on me, expression grim, as if she disapproved of the weather. She'd never liked being cold.

I frowned back, realising something was off.

Cold.

Why could I feel a breeze running through the Folly? All the windows should be shut, unless...

Where was Dad?

The old familiar anxiety gripped me. I remembered what he said about assaulting a police officer so he could get back into prison. I wondered what his state of mind was, if he was truly as miserable on the inside as I suspected. Since our move to the Folly I had nursed a growing notion that mentally, Dad was not alright. Not that he ever communicated this to me, it was just a gut feeling. A tightness between his eyes that never seemed to go away. A tense way of holding himself, as if he were still taking up too much space in a room. Lines around the corners of his mouth. The sad slump of his chin.

I jerked out of the armchair and lurched up the stairs to Dad's bedroom, where my suspicions were confirmed. His door swung open, banging loudly against the Folly wall, and I saw rain sheeting into his room and down onto his bed, for he had opened the trapdoor in his ceiling, the stupid man, he had opened it and gone out onto the platform on top of the tower in the middle of a howling gale and rainstorm.

I thought then that Dad was dead, that this was it. This was how he had chosen to go, just like the author lady. The Folly had cast its spell, and reaped another soul.

However on scrambling up the small folding ladder, heart pounding in my chest, Dad's name falling from my lips urgent and shrill, I found him alive, determinedly so. He stood on top of the Folly, drenched, facing the storm head on, clutching the crenels stoically for all the world as if he were the captain of a ship out at sea, a ship he was trying to steer into safe waters. He gripped the slick stonework and confronted the furious winds that pummeled him as a man would pummel a punching bag with his fists, buffeting him and trying to break him in half, but Dad held his ground, his clothes sodden, his skin shining wet. Eyes closed, he seemed almost in a state of reverie, mouth hanging open, his body vibrating against gusts of angry air that must have been moving at ninety miles an hour, and I screamed at him to come inside, but he didn't hear me above the howling storm dog in his ears.

"Dad!" I shrieked again as the wind ripped at my hair and rain stung my skin. "What are you doing?! You're going to get hurt!"

He still couldn't hear, face turned to the tumult, so I hoisted myself up carefully onto the platform and edged slowly across to him until I could take a hold of his elbow and shake him, hard. The wind nearly knocked me off my own feet, which slithered about on the rain-slicked platform, and I felt a sudden rage move in me, for why should I have to risk breaking my neck like this? What idiocy did I have to compensate for now? When was it my turn to be the child again, instead of the sensible parent?

"Dad!" I screamed again, furious with him now. "For God's sake, what are you *doing*?"

His eyes snapped open, and he finally looked at me. In that moment, I did not know him, so wildly blank and hostile was the expression on his face. It was an animal expression, one lacking in anything markedly reasoned or restrained, as if all human sentiment and constraint had slipped out of his body and mind and left behind only the husk, with its instinctive, base needs and wants and motivations, and he suddenly frightened me, so I fell back half a step, although I kept a hold of his elbow.

"I'm remembering how to be alive!" he shouted then, with force, but his face was the opposite of alive. It was an automaton face, a moulded facsimile face. I could see blood on his lips: his gums were still infected, or maybe he'd bitten himself.

I didn't know what to say. I just needed him to come inside before one of us got hurt.

Of course. It hit me as I floundered and shivered in the sideways rain. He had not seen a storm for a long time. It must be exciting for him.

I didn't much care.

"Come inside, Dad! *Now!*"

The spell broke. The crazy blankness melted from his face. A small, reluctant life-light returned to his eyes. He did not argue, simply let go of the crenellations. As he did so, a bolt of lightning came from the sky and I heard it, fizzing, I *saw* it, a blinding slice of light just behind Dad's head, and it was suddenly like I was looking at one of the paintings in the living room downstairs: Dad illuminated on the rain-lashed tower, lightning playing about him, trying to find release by grounding, the electric discharge desperately seeking a home, as we all were, but finding nothing to attach itself to. Dad's face was a picture of shock and exhilaration, and I pulled hard to get him away from the lightning bolt, which dissipated a second later, and together, we scrambled back down through the hatch into Dad's bedroom, panting and shivering, and secured the trap-door, ramming its bolt home with numb, wet fingers.

Soaked to the bone and trembling with cold, we stood in a spreading puddle in his room, which I hoped would not leak through the carpeted floor and any underlay and penetrate my ceiling and leak down to the next floor. Apart from the repair bill this would incur, I began to nurse a wild vision of my bed collapsing through rotting, sodden floorboards, falling with me still in the bed, fast asleep as it crashed down through level after level until hitting the bottom in a large, wet pulp of mattress and bed sheets and limbs and hair and ceiling plaster and...

"What were you *thinking*?" I yelled, chest still heaving from adrenaline and the leftover dregs of fear. "Don't you know how dangerous that was? Dad! Look at me!"

Before he could answer, the sound of smashing glass came to us up the Folly stairwell. As we were in the topmost room of the tower, there was only one way to go to investigate: down.

We found the source of the noise back in the living room. Broken glass and whipping rain greeted us where it shouldn't have. Lying amongst the glass shards on the rug in the middle of the round room, a bird, dying, its wings broken. It was a tern, a small black and white seabird, one of my favourites. I saw red on the glass and on the rug. I felt raging heat go through me suddenly, a sure sign I was about to vomit. I couldn't look at blood on a carpeted surface and not think about Mum.

I turned away, my hand clamped to my mouth. Dad stood there, observing the mess, and the wildness was still in his eyes.

"Dad, it's dying," I said weakly. "Put it outside, please."

"It's in pain," he replied in a sotto voice I didn't like. "It needs putting out of its misery."

And he snatched up the heavy cast iron poker from its stand in the fireplace, raising it above his head, high, swift, sure.

He was going to smash the bird's head in, right then and there on the rug in front of me.

His face at that moment was a picture of sheer intent.

Focused, deadly.

Murderous.

I had never seen him like that before.

Had Mum?

"Dad!" I squealed, horrified. "Not in the house! Jesus!"

The bird squawked and thumped its shattered wings pitifully against the rug. Dad looked at me, inscrutable.

Then he scooped up the bird and took it downstairs, along with the poker.

I set about finding something to cover the broken window with—cardboard, plastic, wood—but my brain struggled to make sense of the task. I was deeply shaken. None of this was working out the way I had planned it, the way I had hoped. Meanwhile, broken glass and feathers and blood were scattered everywhere, and the rain was still hurtling in through the shattered aperture the bird had left.

I finally spotted an old packing crate leaning against the wall, which I flattened, thinking to gaffer tape it to the window frame. Dad had brought several rolls of the stuff with him, as it had always been his go-to, his fix-all.

I was about to cover the smashed porthole when I caught a glimpse of my father through the jagged hole in the glass. He stood near the foot of the Folly in the driving, furious rain. The bird was on the ground by his feet, and Dad was beating it violently with the poker, over and over again, not to kill it, not to put it out of its misery, but to smash the poor creature into a pulp of feathers and gore, to obliterate it from existence. Watching him batter the bird to a flattened, pink mess as lightning flashed once more in the sky above made me see him for the first time as all those other people must have seen him after Mum died, for he looked like a murderer, he looked vile, and dangerous, and once I saw him like that, it was difficult to unsee, an impossible image to shake, even though it was my dad, and I knew he was not like that, not really. How could he be? He was my *dad*. He loved me, and I loved him.

But doubt crept into my heart. I found I was not ready for it.

I blotted him out with the packing crate and sealed the edges of the window with layer upon layer of thick, heavy duty tape, plastering it on as thickly as if I were sealing the gaps around my own heart.

ELEVEN

The following day, I had wet clothes to dry. There was a small washing line strung up a few yards from the front door of the Folly. I did a load of laundry, including the blood-splattered rug and our rain-sodden clothes, and hung everything out, for the weather had reverted to clear blue skies, a light breeze, and strong sunshine, as if the storm had not even happened.

I thought about Mum as I pegged each item of clothing to the line, feeling the wind tug and play with the garments as soon as they were aloft. She had a very specific way of hanging clothes out: socks, matched in pairs, attached to the line by one clothespin, trousers hung upside down by their ankles, two clothespins, shirts right side up by the cuffs of the sleeves, two

clothespins, sweaters by the bottom hem, three clothespins to stop the wool from losing its shape... I remembered all of this as I tried to get through the chore as
quickly as possible, because I had always hated laundry,
and always would. My mother's way might have been
better, but it took twice as long, so I ignored her method
and haphazardly attached the washing to the line in the
quickest way I could. I felt heavy in my mind and body
and wanted to take a walk to refresh myself. But chores
first, or the clothes would never dry in time.

The washing dealt with, I passed by a misshapen
lump of mashed bird flesh and feathers on my way to
return the laundry basket to its home under the foot of
the staircase. The beady, accusing eye of the tern stared
at me from where it nudged up against its splintered
beak. I remembered Dad with his poker, working fever-
ishly. I wondered where the murder weapon was now.
Had he put it back in the hearth? Had he wiped it, at
least?

I put this to the back of my mind like a good girl,
and went for a walk.

A dusty, slender path led me to the end of the peninsula, where the hooked part of the spit of land dipped
down. I could see, as I got closer to the edge than I ever
had before, that there was a sizable hollow in the crook
of this hook, a hollow I had not noticed before. In that
hollow, a series of man-made niches were hewn into the

hard, unforgiving rock. Like handholds, or footholds. Had someone been climbing here? I could see no sign of the tell-tale steel belay hook.

I leaned over as far as I dared to get a better look. The niches went halfway down the cliff and then seemed to stop at an overhang.

Is there an old smuggler's cave down there? I wondered. A natural fissure in the rocks?

I didn't have the guts to climb down and find out, but I didn't need to: a rush of swallows flew out of the side of the cliff, and I knew there must be a cave decorated with dozens of swallow's nests, for they liked to build their sticky, papery dens inside of things, under cover. I imagined a large, craggy space just out of sight, deep and dark and damp. Why else would there be niches carved into the rock, unless they led somewhere?

It made me a little uneasy to think about. If there was a cave, was someone living in it? The niche-steps looked clean and worn, as if well used. Was this where the local teens came to smoke pot and have sex? I didn't like that idea. I was beginning to feel fiercely protective of the Folly and the land attached to it. It was our space, our private space. I didn't want to share it with anyone: death tourists, teenagers, or frightening, bald-headed strangers.

I returned to the Folly on a different path to the route I usually took, skirting around the edges of the green plain and meandering instead through the small wooded strip that sheltered the tower from the mainland. This put the front door and the washing line and the dead bird on the opposite side of the structure from me, so it was not until I rounded the foot of the Folly and came face to face with the stranger casually rearranging my laundry on the line, that I knew anything was wrong.

He was wearing an apron this time, tied tight over his midriff. It had yellow and red flowers on it and the words HEAD CHEF, embroidered in red cotton.

I froze mid-step.

"Hello, love," the stranger said in that odd, soft voice of his. He drew out the syllable at the end of *hello*, just like Mum used to do.

Mum also had an apron just like the one he wore. I had given it to her as a gift years ago for her birthday. I had put the thing in storage after her death, reluctant to throw it out, but then I'd had a change of heart and donated her entire wardrobe to a second-hand clothing shop in the city.

I stood, immobilized by abject confusion and fear as the man who spoke in my mother's voice corrected my sloppy laundry hanging. He carefully pinned each item the right way up, just the way Mum had always done. I watched him pair the socks together and peg them in place with a single clothespin. I watched him turn the sweater upside down and hang it by the long hem. Three clothespins. I watched him upend Dad's trousers and jeans, clip them by the ankles to the line.

I thought about yelling at the man to scare him off, then I thought about running inside and calling the police, but neither of those things seemed appropriate, or feasible, the longer I stood there. For one, my phone was out of battery, charging in my bedroom, and for two, my throat had seized up. I was incapable of letting loose anything louder than a whisper or a rasp.

So instead, without fully understanding why, I decided to indulge the man. Clearly, he was not a complete stranger. He must have known my mother when she was alive. This harassment was an elaborate prank, perhaps because he hated my dad for what he thought had been done to her. Perhaps because he, like so many others, had been swept up by the trial and poisoned by it. I had never really appreciated the full capability of the human brain to become corrupted by news coverage until I had become the daughter of an accused man.

Whatever his motivations, if this man wanted to fuck with my head, he was going to have to try harder. I was patient and very good at playing other people's games. I had developed an expertise for both while campaigning for Dad's release.

I took a deep breath, unclenched my fists. Forced my voice out into the open with some difficulty.

"Hello, Mum," I said, behaving as if she were actually standing there, rearranging the laundry for me.

"Nice walk?" the man replied, and it was uncanny, I had to give him that. The more I heard him speak, the more he sounded like her. He had done his homework.

"I found some steps leading down to a cave. Is that where you live?"

The man shook his head and gave me a quizzical look. "What are you talking about? What cave?"

"The cave down there, at the tip of the peninsula. On the side of the cliff. Is that where you've been hiding?" I struggled to keep my voice calm and as neutral as possible.

The man shook his head indulgently. "Honestly, love, you do come up with some nonsense sometimes. I don't live in a cave. I live here, with you and Dad. Just like a family is supposed to."

With those last words, the strange bald-headed man stopped fiddling with the laundry. I had only a split second to understand his intentions before he ran over to me, so quickly and with such a wild burst of unnatural speed that I had no time to turn tail and run myself. He was upon me before I could blink. Up close, his eyes were blood red around the pupils, which were dilated. Was he on something? Medication? Speed? Dried spittle caked the corners of his lips. His teeth were brown and in bad condition.

The man gripped me by the shoulders and leaned his head into my face, pushing his nose hard into mine, so hard it hurt. A blinding pain shot through my forehead. Blood began dripping from my left nostril, warm and salty. It trickled into my mouth.

I struggled, but the stranger held me tight and fast.

"JUST LIKE A FAMILY IS SUPPOSED TO!" he shrieked, full into my face, and for a second, I heard not one voice, but two, intertwined, like a vine strangling a rose. I could smell fish and stale coffee on his breath. And something else.

Something that smelled like...

Mum's perfume. Hiding, under the stench.

Patchouli and jasmine, her favourite.

Dad would buy her a new bottle every year.

I screamed in terror.

The man screamed back, the sound dissolving into a wail and then at last into a horrible, chuckling laugh.

Then the stranger impersonating my mother let go of me. He ran off to the end of the peninsula, where he lowered himself deftly over the cliff edge and disappeared. He moved so quickly I had trouble keeping up with his movements, which was the most frightening thing about him. His speed. Like a spider darting across a web. It was inconceivable that a man of his size and build could shift like that. One second he was there, thundering along the path, the next...

He was gone. Presumably, he had scrambled all the way down the cliff face using the carved niches. He did live in the cave, of that I was now certain. What I could do with that information, I didn't know. Give it to the police? And say what, we were being harassed by a man who thought he was my dead mother? Please could we get a restraining order for the six-foot-four guy in the flowery apron?

No, that wouldn't work. They would laugh at us. Wouldn't they? I didn't trust the police much, not after everything that had happened with Dad's trial.

Should I still call them, though?

No. Not now. Not now.

Now?

No, I couldn't.

I couldn't think straight.

I could barely breathe.

I could taste the man's foul breath on my tongue.

His/her words rang in my ears.

Shocked and dazed, I let my legs fold, and sat heavily down on the grass, where I remained, gazing at the flapping laundry, the shirts that looked like fluttering ghosts, the bloodstained rug, the sweaters, hung upside down, just the way Mum liked, until Dad found me.

TWELVE

I continued to debate calling the police for a good, long while. In the end, Dad made the decision where I could not: he had no desire to jeopardise our new life any further than it already was. Neither of us wanted to risk the arrangement we had in place. Neither of us wanted to draw attention to ourselves, or suffer the possibility of our whereabouts leaking to the media, who would collectively fall over themselves for an exclusive scoop on the wife-killer who now lived in the infamous Wailing Pillar of lore, not to mention the added jus of the possessed, pinny-wearing man who stalked him and his long-suffering sap of a daughter, until they lost interest and moved onto some other tawdry story.

Neither of us could afford to move again, or rent someplace else.

Besides, we were dubious about how seriously we would be taken by the police, given the nature of our complaint. All the stranger had done, after all, was loiter and rearrange some laundry. Hardly cause for arrest.

It proved easier, all things measured and weighed, to stay quiet than to speak out.

So, quiet we kept. We formed an odd pact of silence about the stranger, but Dad started patrolling the Folly like a guard on duty, gripping the poker by his side wherever he went.

I retreated into baking for comfort. I made apple pie, for we had apples to use up. I had naively asked the owner to add more to our grocery order in the hope I could force some nutrition into Dad, but they had sat ignored and unloved in a fruit bowl to the point of going brown and soft in places. I could salvage them with cinnamon and cloves, and hope there was some residual goodness after, although the chances of that were slim, for Dad liked pie served with custard, and ice cream sometimes, on the side. He also liked the pastry thick and glazed with egg and sprinkled with brown sugar. Still, apples. And health concerns aside, I wanted to make the damn pie because it felt like a safe, wholesome thing to do, and that was, after all, why I had

moved us out here. For safety. For normalcy. For whole-
someness.

I didn't register until halfway through mixing the
short-crust pastry with cold water and a pastry knife that
apple pie was Mum's favourite recipe. She would make it
on a Saturday morning, and today—I had to double
check, for time had lost a lot of its meaning at the Folly
—was, indeed, Saturday.

Grief, I was still discovering, was pernicious. Even all
these years later. It stalked me with eyes full of lessons
yet to be learned, and I was so oblivious to its presence it
found me easy prey. I only had myself to blame for this:
I had been so intent on my father, on freeing him, fixing
him, healing him, that I had neglected my own feelings.
Now, my body was taking charge, walking me along the
path to acceptance without my full consent or apprecia-
tion. *Funny how the brain works,* I thought, as I worked
the lardy pastry crumbs into a thick ball with the knife. I
was baking because I was grieving, still trying to get back
to the real memories of my mother. The good
memories.

And, I had to admit, to get further away from the
awful imagery of a tall, bald man mimicking my mother's voice. Reorganising our laundry. Twirling an imaginary strand of hair, round and around and around.

Gripping me with the strength of ten men, forcing
his face into mine.

I could remember exactly how his skin had felt, exactly how he had smelled.

If he showed up again, I *would* call the police, I decided, despite what Dad said. I *would* take the risk. The press could go fuck themselves. Let them write what they wanted. As long as Dad and I were safe. I had fought for this new life, and I was not going to lose it to a performative grudge that had nothing to do with anything real, or true, or present. For I had decided that this was the stranger's motivation: revenge. He must have been an old friend of Mum's, someone with a vested interest in her case. The nagging familiarity of his features lent weight to this theory. So did the memory of Dad lying about having never met the man before. Maybe the stranger was a childhood friend Mum had lost touch with, or an old boyfriend.

It didn't matter. I didn't care why the man was harassing us. I just needed him to go away. I needed to feel safe.

But would we ever be safe, really? This thought was heavy, like wet pastry in a bowl. With the past always there, on record the way it was?

I glanced out the kitchen porthole window and spotted Dad navigating the path that led to the cliffs. He was limping a little. This was because he had the iron poker threaded through his belt at his hip, like a sword in a scabbard. He had the binoculars with him too, and a notebook, a half-hearted disguise for his real mission: to check out the cave. I didn't want him to go down there, had pleaded with him to stay away, but Dad was single-minded. I did not think him agile enough to get down the carved niche ladder, but maybe he thought he could act as a deterrent, mark his territory somehow. It was interesting, watching him patrol. It made me think he had become as protective of our new home as I had.

The Folly was ours, and we would not be run out of it.

I kept Dad in sight as I absentmindedly sliced at the freshly formed pastry in the bowl. I still could not get used to how diminished the formerly comforting bulk of him was. He walked with purpose along the cliff edge, and seemed almost gaunt, from my perspective up in the Folly. Odd how he seemed to suit the wild, craggy setting though: like a character from one of the worn, tattered novels that sat on the fireplace mantle in our living room, a gift from the owner. I had not been able to focus much on reading since I had arrived, but if we could get over the hurdle of this strange period of transition, I might pick one up. Reading was supposed to be a relaxing pastime. Mum had always loved a good novel. She had read religiously every night before bed, using a special little clip-light clamped to the book's spine so she didn't keep Dad awake. It was not unusual for her to get through two books or more a week.

I continued to stab at the pastry, painfully aware that mine had never been up to Mum's standard. A great and unexpected anguish built up in the space behind my lungs, viciously forcing the breath out of me. I suddenly imagined her leaning over my shoulder, telling me how to hold the knife, telling me to use different temperature water, telling me not to overwork the pastry or use my hands too much, her breath like dead fish and patchouli, her hair falling out until she was completely bald, her brains running down her face and dripping off her chin —did she fall or was she pushed?—and I knew I had it all mixed up, all the different memories of her, real or otherwise, mixed up like congealed lard and butter and flour and the wrong temperature water, and just like that, I lost her, all over again. I lost what had made her my mum, and thanks to the stranger, I was now also afraid of her memory.

I was afraid of my own dead mother.

And Dad, too, after the bird. I didn't want to admit that to myself, but it was true.

This realisation upset me hugely. For the first time in a long time, I found myself crying, my tears dripping into the pastry.

Oh well, the recipe asked for a pinch of salt, I told myself, and I tried to wipe my face, forgetting that my hands were covered in clumped flour, because I hadn't followed Mum's instructions, and I'd used my hands, so

I ended up making a sticky, pasty mess of myself, which made me cry even more. I was a disgrace, Mum would have said, shaking her head and rushing in to help. She had always been a tidy baker, a clean-up-as-you-go type, the type that measured things precisely and timed things exactly, whereas I always threw things into a bowl like a slob and hoped for the best.

Shoulders heaving, sight clouded, I reached out for a towel to wipe my hands and knocked a jug of water over myself instead. Then, as I flailed about trying to mop up the mess, I upended a cup of whisked egg yolks I'd put to one side to glaze the pie lid with. I felt both water and egg seep into my clothes and spread across my crotch and thought, *Of course. Of course.*

A vivid flashback of Dad beating the seabird to a red, raw mess crawled into my mind, where muddled memories of Mum had been hurting my brain only moments before. A headache made its presence known, throbbing along my brow bone and up my temples.

I was beginning to feel very, very defeated.

I was trying my best, wasn't I?

Couldn't they see that?

I was trying my best to make this all work.

I cast a final despairing look at Dad, who had almost reached the niches in the cliff, and thought: *Fine. Do what you want, then. Be it on your head.*

Then I went to my bedroom to strip off my sodden

clothes and change into clean ones. On the way, I passed through our tiny circular bathroom and washed my hands free from the clumped flour and fat. I scrubbed at my skin longer than was necessary, using a nail brush until my hands were raw and red. I wasn't sure what I was trying to wash away, in truth: the baking detritus, or the growing sensation of despair creeping along my flesh.

While I was changing, which took longer than I wanted because I had not yet finished putting away yesterday's laundry—I didn't really want to touch it, truth be told, and was considering re-washing it—I heard clattering and movement in the kitchen down below.

Dad, returned, already? And sticking his nose, and fingers, no doubt, into my business.

Typical.

"Don't interfere with the pie!" I yelled down the stairs to him. "I haven't finished yet!"

More clattering, the definitive thump and clack of the large pastry bowl being handled.

How could Dad have gotten back here so quickly? I looked out my bedroom window, puzzled.

There he was. At the cliff edge, looking down at the carved niches, poker in hand.

I froze.

More clattering downstairs.

Then humming. A song.

Mum's favourite song.

"Waterloo" by ABBA.

She had always been tone-deaf, and whoever was humming was, too.

I had a good idea that I knew who.

He's inside, I thought, frantically. *He's inside our fucking tower!*

I yanked a fresh pair of jeans up and fastened them with shaking hands.

The humming grew louder and more enthusiastic.

Then I opened my bedroom window, still topless apart from my bra, and I yanked a white pillowcase from my bed, waving it frantically out the round window to get Dad's attention. I didn't know Morse code, but I knew this was close enough. *S.O.S,* I thought I waved, *S.O.S!* Or at least that was my intention. My arm stretched awkwardly out of the narrow porthole, and the pillowcase flapped in the breeze. Had Dad seen it? Would it work?

I kept waving, and then heard a crash downstairs. The pastry bowl had shattered. Had to be. It was the only thing in the kitchen substantial enough to make such a solid, destructive noise.

I tried one last desperate signal, and I thought, although I couldn't be entirely sure at this distance, that

Dad turned, saw me, but I didn't have time to contemplate it further.

I turned, rammed a shirt down over my head, looked about me for a weapon. The only thing I could find was the bedside table lamp, which I unplugged, wrapping the cable around and around my arm for extra protection, the plug nestling in the palm of my hand, pins up, the lamp itself brandished in the other hand, and crept stealthily down the stairs, thinking we should have called the police, I knew we should have called the fucking police, to find the bald-headed stranger in my kitchen, on his knees, picking up fragments of shattered pastry bowl, still humming "Waterloo." The lyrics slipped out from between cracked lips—"I was forsaken, you won the war."—and I wanted to cry all over again, except I was burning out of emotion and fast becoming an empty vessel, a hollow ship, scuttled and left for driftwood, so instead I stood in the doorway and asked, as politely as I knew how, what the fuck he was doing in my house.

"Language, please," the stranger replied without looking up. He neatly placed all the broken shards of the bowl on a newspaper sheet and proceeded to wrap them up into a tidy, safe package.

He was wearing the apron again, I saw. HEAD CHEF. And slippers this time. Leather-soled slippers with a fur trim. The exact type Mum had coveted. There was a particular brand she liked that you didn't find in many places. If I saw them in a shop, I bought two pairs, because they were so hard to come by. She always used to say it felt like wearing clouds on her feet.

"Get out," I replied as firmly as I knew how.

"Don't be ridiculous," he admonished, smoothly rising to his feet. His height surprised me every time. There was stubble on his chin, peppered with grey. His eyebrows were thick and unkempt and very, very dark.

His eyes were the same colour as my mother's.

"Why are you doing this?" I asked, feeling faint. I was so tired, I just wanted peace.

"You never did learn to tidy up as you went along, did you? This is exactly why I taught you to. Now look at all this mess."

"You need to get out, before I call the police. You can't be here. You're trespassing."

"And how many times did I tell you to mix the cinnamon in with the pastry mix? It gives it a kick, I told you. And a pinch of nutmeg with *two* pinches of salt, not one."

"If you don't get out, I am going to have to make you. You're intruding on private property. I can have the police here in moments." I knew that wasn't true. I would have to take my phone, which was on the counter behind the man, up to the top floor of the Folly to get enough signal to call, and we both knew I wouldn't be able to reach it before he could.

The futility of my situation gave me renewed clarity. I decided once again that talking was better than threatening, so I swallowed my rage and fear and tried reasoning with the stranger for the second time that week.

"I'm not sure what you think you're achieving here, but Dad did nothing wrong, despite what you think," I said, my voice unsteady.

He looked up at me. For a fleeting second, I saw Mum's face looking out of his strange, craggy visage. I gasped.

How could that be?

Was my mind collapsing completely?

"Is that right?" Mum replied, and I knew that expression. It was the expression she had always used when she'd known, deep down, that she was right when someone else was wrong.

Then her countenance morphed back to the stranger's features and a series of twitches and odd, staccato facial tics followed, suggesting the stranger was struggling with something monumental.

I persisted even as every nerve in my body was telling me to run.

"We proved it in a court of law." I stared him down doggedly. "There was not enough substantial evidence to convict him in the first place. The police mishandled his case. It was a mistrial. He did nothing wrong. We... we proved it! It was an accident! He did nothing wrong!" I felt myself become more desperate as the words came out of me.

Who was I trying to convince?

Him?

Myself?

Or Mum?

The stranger dusted his own floury hands on his apron, using the same method Mum had always used: wipe the backs, then the fronts, then each finger individually, a little baking ritual, for she had been like that, always needing to keep her hands busy. She had been full of nervous, efficient energy from the moment she woke up to the moment she fell asleep with her book on her face.

"Define wrong," the bald-headed man said then, sounding more baritone, and was that a hint of a Cornish accent leaking through?

I couldn't take it anymore, this invasion, this infection of my hopeful new life, this horrible, unexpected, unwanted intrusion that was not only ruining my present, my future, but was systematically destroying my past, sacred remembrances now turning to hatred and fear, meaning I felt orphaned all over again, and forcing me to realise how deeply, how desperately, how fundamentally alone I was, even with Dad only just outside, because what all children really wanted was their mother, when it came down to the bare truth of the matter. I wanted my mum, my *real* mum, not this perverted, cruel mannequin version of her. I wanted her to wrap me up in her strong arms and stroke my hair like she used to when I was a child. I wanted it so much I could have ripped all of my own hair out in great, vicious chunks right then and there on the spot. My fingers went to my head, old habits die hard, but I remembered I'd cut it all short for this very reason.

So instead, I pounded the sides of my skull with my fists in futile agony and screamed.

"What do you want!?" I yelled. "*What?* He served his time! He deserves a second chance!"

"He served time," the man replied, blinking as if waking and seeing the light of a new day. "But did he serve enough?"

"What are you talking about?" I stared at him. Were his eyes changing colour?

"Ask him about 1976."

"What about 1976?"

But the man's face crumpled into a mess of confusion and panic as he seemed to become newly aware of his surroundings. He looked at his hands, the apron, the slippers, the kitchen, and then, at last, at me.

"Who the fuck are you?" he cried. Then his eyes

rolled back in his skull, and he crumpled to the floor, on which there was barely enough space to accommodate him, and he began to fit, seizures violently contorting his huge frame as I stood there and watched in abject shock and wondered distantly, through a haze of disbelief, if he was about to die right there in front of me.

It was at this point that Dad stumbled up the stairs, poker held out before him, breath ragged with panic, calling out my name. He lurched to a clumsy halt when he saw me in the doorway of the kitchen, watching help-lessly as the huge paroxysmal man on the floor went slowly purple. The stranger was choking on something, I realised. I could see his mouth working around some sort of large mass obstructing his airways, but I wasn't about to get anywhere near him to see what it was.

The man continued to convulse, and I could have sworn I heard bone cracking.

"Call an ambulance?" Dad said faintly.

"I suppose...I suppose we should." But I didn't move. I couldn't. I could barely feel my own skin on my bones. Dad reached around me, over the man, and snatched my phone from the counter. He stabbed at the keypad three times with a finger, then held it to his ear.

Meanwhile, the man on the floor flipped over, coughing, hacking, retching, choking. My hand went to my own throat, almost a show of sympathy. It was utterly mesmerising, I discovered, watching someone die. Captivating, in the worst possible way. I had only ever seen the aftermath, not the procedure. I found the latter almost fascinating, as it progressed.

"I can't get a dial tone!" Dad cried, and the look on his face woke me up.

If another dead body were to be found in another house Dad lived in, well...

"Go up to the roof!" I shouted, finally preparing myself to kneel down and help the stranger, even if that meant CPR or sticking my fingers in his throat to clear his airway and help him to breathe, but at that point, the man on the floor strained and heaved and arched his back like a sick cat, and vomited up a huge, matted clump of hair, hair that was the same colour and consistency and texture as my mother's hair.

Purged—were his eyes a different colour again?—the man smiled, and in Mum's voice, he crooned:

"Yes, go up to the roof, Owen."

Dad went completely white. That voice.

There was no denying it, not anymore.

It was impossible, but it was her.

Not just a man mimicking her, but her real voice, spilling from his mouth like a noxious cloud of cigarette smoke.

My father bolted up the stairs. Not to help, but to escape.

I had never seen him move so fast.

The man on the floor roared, rose in one fluid motion, pushed me violently to one side, and ran after him.

I heard footsteps hammering on the stairs: one set, a second set clattering after the first. A corkscrewed chase, a dangerous pursuit, for it was easy to slip on the cast iron steps, slip and tumble from the top of the tower all the way to the very bottom. My thoughts spiraled like the metal steps.

Blood and brains on a deep pile carpet. Scrape it off with your fingernail, it's the only way. Try not to think about the person the dried matter had been, try not to imagine tiny fragments of her soul, her essence, under your fingernails, try not to lift your hand to your mouth in a daze of horror and clean the gunk from underneath each nail with the edges of your teeth, try not to taste, to savour, to swallow, try...try...

Mum, I miss you...

I followed, using the rail to haul myself up two steps at a time, urging my body to move faster than it physically could, hearing the trapdoor in Dad's room clang down, hearing more steps on rungs, feeling the sea air funnel down the stairway, reaching the top of the Folly, dragging myself through the portal in just enough time to see Dad, back to the crenellations, clinging on once more for dear life, only there was no storm this time, only the bald man, who stood on the very lip of the

Folly's edge, or rather, stood with one foot in a crenel, the other up on a merlon—for that was what Dad told me they were called, the highs and lows, crenels and merlons—and he swayed about unsteadily in the wind, waited for me to surface, and said in Mum's teasing, yet matter of fact way:

"You always were two minutes late to every party, Morgan."

Then he turned away from me. Sunlight beat down on his polished egg head. I saw a fishing boat chug along at speed on the horizon. Could they see us? Doubtful, they had work to do. No reason to train their eyes this way. Nobody else in the world was witness to this peculiar drama, only the birds in the sky, and they didn't much care.

"Ask your Dad about 1976," my mother's voice said, and then she, or he, or both of them, jumped off the Folly tower top.

Dad and I both hurled ourselves at the space where the man had been, reaching out to grab, to stop, to save, but it was too late. We heard the thud of impact. We heard the cry of seagulls, who took no hesitation in swooping down, for there was fresh meat to be pecked at.

Shaking in horror, we craned our heads over the Folly edge and looked down.

The bald-headed man lay spread-eagled on his back,

like the bird that still lay mashed on the grass nearby. A bright fan of blood spread around his body like a crimson nimbus, catching the sunlight. I could see bits of him glistening like obscene jewels. I could not separate the two bodies out in my mind, human, bird, and this made me shy away from Dad without even knowing what I was doing. I simply had a sudden and overwhelming knee-jerk need to get away from my father. I managed to control this urge as best I could, telling myself that Dad was not the enemy, no matter how much he suddenly made my skin crawl.

I ground my fingernails into the stone merlons and forced myself to remain by his side as I tried to process what had just happened. My entire body had gone cold with shock, and I heard a gathering sound in my ears, not unlike the roaring of the ocean.

Why had the man jumped?

It didn't make sense. Why go to such great lengths to mess with us, play games with us, if the plan was to jump all along?

"He's getting up," Dad croaked, in an awful whisper, and at first that statement made no sense, but then I saw that he was right.

In disbelief, I watched as the bald man slowly climbed to his feet. Or rather, foot, his left foot. His right was a useless flapping thing, the leg shattered and twisted.

"How is he still alive?" I breathed.

Nobody should be able to survive a fall from that height.

Nobody.

The man, who was red all over now, straightened. He reminded me of a scarecrow mounted on a pole, stuffing leaking out where birds had pecked at him. Then, in a tortured display of crazed, wholly uncoordinated animation, he began to shuffle off in the direction of the cave. His ruined leg trailed behind him like a fleshy scarf, and I saw, even from where I stood, high up, the sharp protrusions of bone that pierced his skin. I remembered hugging Dad, fresh out of prison, hard nubs of malnutrition poking into me where there should have been warm, soft cushions of flesh. *We are all just a collection of bones*, I thought, wondering if I had finally snapped beyond repair. *Are her bones still comfortable? She was always so particular about how she arranged herself, so particular...*

Watching the man go rewired something inside me. It changed me in the same way that finding my own mother's dead body at the bottom of the stairs had changed me. The stranger's jerky, tortured forward march reminded me of stop-motion models mimicking stilted approximations of human movement in lurid, brightly saturated technicolour movies from the sixties. It didn't seem human: rather, the bone collection heaved itself along by sheer force of will, this assortment of organs and limbs and ragged, trailing appendages. The sky was now filled with seabirds, with ravenous gulls, all diving and ducking and tugging at parts of the useless leg as the man stumbled on toward the cliff edge.

I felt hot, and sweaty, and sick.

How was he even staying upright?

Was my mother keeping his body going?

It seemed like something she would be able to do. She had been ever persistent, ever stubborn.

But if that were the case, why had she not kept *herself* alive after her own fall?

If physical pain was no barrier for her, why leave me alone the way she did?

Why abandon me?

I would not have minded the state of her body, had her essence remained. We could have talked, we could have made it work somehow.

What was I thinking?

I wondered again if, perhaps, I was actually going mad.

Could I still taste her on my teeth?

The man dragged himself off to his cave on the tip of the peninsula, still harassed by a screeching cloud of birds, but I could watch no more.

I went down to my room, feeling dizzy and sick, inching my way with exaggerated care, step by step, gripping the handrail, leaving Dad alone on the tower top. I shut my bedroom door, climbed into bed, pulled the covers up over my head, and I stayed there, unmoving, for two days and three nights.

Dad didn't call the police, or an ambulance, but then I hadn't expected him to. Instead, he tried to help by baking the unfinished apple pie for me on the second day. He brought it to me, limp and undercooked, in a bowl, begging me to get up, to eat something.

Listlessly, I did as I was told and pressed the spoon into the pale, soggy shortcrust, brought up a mouthful of stewed apple and raw pastry. I dutifully shovelled it into my mouth, trying not to grimace at the consistency, which was like baby food. I didn't feel as if I would ever be hungry again.

Especially when, frowning, I stopped mid-chew, and extricated something long, thick, and uncomfortable from my mouth.

One of Mum's hairs.

I did not finish the pie.

THIRTEEN

We didn't see the man again after that. I wondered if he had crawled into his cave and died, which seemed a realistic outcome, given the state of him. Animated or not, possessed or otherwise, no one could survive a fall from even half as high up without hospital treatment. Adrenaline would only have carried him so far. Sepsis, infection, shock... they would all have been waiting for him in the wings, a deadly trio. I had learned from bitter experience how fragile the human body really was. Was he down there in that unseen rocky cleft, rotting away in the briny sea air? Did he have family? Shouldn't we tell someone?

And what about what lived *inside* his body? Was that dead by now, too?

Whether it was my mother, or simple malice, a thirst for revenge, a terrible, terrible prank dressed up as "teaching us a lesson," or perhaps a mental disorder, an obsession, a deranged desire to impersonate and perhaps be loved as she was...

Whatever it was, had it died, too?

Regardless, his whereabouts became a mystery, and I hated the lingering threat of him. If he had gone to the cliff wall, or maybe circled round, unseen, to the woods behind us, or maybe even fallen into the sea, or wandered out onto the main road inland, or...whatever, I would have felt better with confirmation of his exact state. Not to mention, there was an injured, probably deceased man out there somewhere. An unpleasant surprise for some other hapless, innocent person to stumble across. Didn't we have a duty to report the accident, at the very least?

Yes.

We did.

We should have reported it.

But we didn't.

Dad didn't want to go back to jail. It was that simple. Because who, after all, would believe in two accidental falls? There wasn't a police officer or judge or jury in the world who would be that impartial to his past history. How did the nursery rhyme go? *Humpty*

*Dumpty sat on a wall, Humpty Dumpty...*of course they wouldn't. They would take one look at his previous conviction, and back inside Dad would go. All the king's horses, and all the king's men, conspiring to put Dad in prison again.

Would that be such a bad thing, Morgan?

I thought this more frequently than I liked admitting to. I was just tired, I reasoned, and disappointed. Things weren't exactly working out the way I'd planned.

Maybe it *would* be better, if he went back inside. Less confusing. For both of us.

My own momentary feelings of disloyalty distressed me so much I found it hard to look at Dad, and he noticed this, registered it, and became withdrawn.

Wherever the bald-headed man had gone, neither of us had the courage to seek him out. We were both too world-damaged, too cowardly. Once, we had been decent people, I thought, but now...not even the knowledge of a man dying, troubled and in agony, somewhere on the peninsula, could prompt us out of ourselves. Instead, we battened down the hatches, turned the heavy iron key in the heavy iron lock on the Folly's front door, and hoped for the best. Because the door had been locked before, and the stranger had still gotten in somehow. Back when his body had been all in one piece.

I was not sure his hands could physically cope with picking a lock, if he wasn't dead, but then, his pulverised form had impossibly dragged itself upright and stumbled off after a fall from a huge height, so what did I know?

Nothing. That much was becoming painfully obvious.

My punishment was fear, anxiety, and paranoia.

It dominated my every waking moment.

Every day, after I managed to haul myself from my bed and back into real life, I waited for an alien sound to ring out in the Folly while Dad was out patrolling the grounds with his poker. Every day I expected to walk into one of the small, round rooms and find the bald-headed man making himself busy in there, dusting, rearranging, cleaning, humming "Waterloo" in a tuneless, cheerful fashion, skin peeling off his festering leg, splintered ribs thrusting out of his clothing like a rotting hull's frame, birds resting on every available body-perch. Every day I braced myself, needlessly as it turned out, for what I might find in the once quaint, seemingly innocent tower I wanted so desperately to call home.

Every day, despite walking everywhere on tiptoe and holding my breath, I found nothing waiting for me. And yet, each time I did *not* have an encounter, it only served to make me more nervous, for it felt like I had unfinished business with Mum.

Perhaps, I began to wonder, as I slowly pieced

together everything that had happened, perhaps she was angry at me.

For defending Dad.

But why?

We had always been a team, our family. That much I had ingrained in my soul. Mum and Dad had been in love, or at least they had loved each other as well as any couple who had been married for a long period of time loved each other. It wasn't all roses and starlight, I knew that, but they supported each other, cared for each other, shared the same outlook on life and goals. They'd had fun together, they'd had a child together. These things bonded couples faster than glue, because bearing the colossal weight of responsibility adhered people to each other, stuck them fast, just like I had been bonded to Dad once the judge's gavel had fallen on him. Immobilised by duty and loyalty and all the things we owed the people who raised us when they needed us, which came sooner with some families than others. I'd had a chance at my own life before then, a glimmer of hope for something other than the quiet, conservative existence I'd lived up until that moment, but Mum had put paid to that when she'd fallen down the stairs.

Which was hardly the point, I knew. The point was, duty and obligation had never seemed to burden Mum, or Dad. With my parents, love had never felt like an encumbrance, not from where I had been watching.

They had enjoyed raising me together. They had enjoyed being my mother, my father, a unit, a team. A family.

So why would Mum be mad at me?

You know why, my warped reflection in the tiny mirror over the tiny bathroom sink would accuse as I cleaned my teeth at night or smoothed cream into my skin.

I would wash this accusation away with tepid water, refusing to acknowledge my reflection further until it behaved itself.

Dad cleaned the mess from the grounds before our next grocery delivery. Not that we had any cause to fear, the driver never came closer than forty yards from the place, but my father knew the stakes, and he wanted to be careful, so he removed every trace of the bald-headed stranger from the grass, swilling the patch where he had landed with boiling water and bleach, which killed the turf off completely, but he didn't mind that so much, because dead grass was easier to explain away than dead flesh. *Rabbits*, he would say. *Dog piss. Kids.* By the time anyone came to check up on us, it would have probably grown back anyway. Secrets were like that. Only visible for a certain brief window of time before they sank to the roots, grew over, became part of a hidden network of tubers and earth. Above them, dead grass, upon which the unsuspecting feet of those who were none the wiser passed. I wondered how many secrets had been washed away in all of human history like that. Even just in the history of the Folly. I knew the author who wrote her book here had been rinsed and sluiced like the bald-headed man. There were more, no doubt. Secrets. Legacies.

I'd had my own secret, which had been carefully disposed of.

I couldn't allow myself to dwell on that too much, I'd done it, I told myself, for the best of reasons. I'd had to focus on Dad. He'd needed my full attention and energy. But I still had moments where I wondered what that secret would look and feel and smell like now, were it lying in my arms instead of...of...

The stone tower would not let me forget, it seemed.

Why?

What was it about this place that was such an echo chamber for loss?

Was it that the ground beneath us was infused with so much blood?

Foundations of pain, of waste, of secrecy, of failure. Such was the platform upon which the Folly stood proud, its black granite blocks rejecting the sun's light and warmth, as if it were ashamed of itself. The structure, as much as any man-made endeavour could, reminded me of Dad, at times. An outlier. A peculiar pillar that only belonged on the fringe. In a town, this building would be incongruous. Here, with only the sea and sky to witness its solitude, it seemed to belong. It was rooted. Rooted with tragedy.

Like Dad.

Like me, for that matter.

After a week had passed, we went down to the niches in the cliff. We waited for high tide, so that if we slipped and fell, we would have a softer and wetter landing than we might have done if it were out. I knew rocks lurked beneath the waves, but water could be forgiving. Exposed Cornish granite was not.

Gingerly, Dad climbed down, taking his time, feeling his way niche by niche. He seemed a good deal more agile than he had a few weeks ago. Perhaps my baking was finally doing the trick. I stood above him, watching with my heart in my mouth as he descended, waiting for a rotting arm to shoot out from the cleft in the rock below and pull my father to his wet, salty death.

The only thing that reached for him were the waves, half-heartedly smacking into the cliff face. Spray heaved itself up into the air, and I worried it would make the clefts slick and slippery, something we hadn't thought about until too late.

But it didn't seem to hamper my father. After only a short while, Dad stood on a slender rock ledge that hadn't been visible to me until he landed on it, so well was it camouflaged.

As I watched, he then disappeared, as if walking

right into the cliff wall like a ghost walking through the walls of a haunted house.

"Dad!" I cried, convinced he'd met foul play.

Dad re-emerged.

"There's no one down here," he called up.

I nearly fainted with relief. No dead body.

"Are you sure?"

"It's perfectly safe. He's been here, but he's gone now. You can come down."

I was hesitant. It looked dangerous.

"Come on, love, we haven't got all day."

He held up a hand, and a look flitted across his face, a look I didn't know.

For a second, I wondered if he was luring me to my death.

I shook myself hard, both physically and mentally. Dad would never hurt me. He loved me. He always had, and nothing about our present situation changed that. Nothing. He was my dad.

Angry with myself, I climbed down backwards, feeling out each wet niche with my foot before putting my weight fully on it. They were deeper footholds than I had prepared for, and the stone was rough and resistant, never slippery. Before I knew it, I was standing on the ledge next to my father, the sea only a little ways below us, birds resting on the surface, riding the swell up and down, up and down. A small, curious face suddenly popped up out of the water, looking up at us from the waves: a seal, lying on its back, huge glossy dark eyes half-closed, nostrils flapping open and closed. It rolled over and slipped back below the surface, flippers disappearing last, and I saw it had long claws on the ends of each one. I'd never known seals had toenails.

I saw a rusted iron chain fixed into the cliffside next to the ledge. It must have been installed a long time ago, for it was covered in green weed and tiny white barnacles that shredded the palm of my hand if I gripped too tight. Still, I clung to it. The ledge was extremely narrow, and it would not take much to topple sideways, launching myself into the sea below. I could swim, but the true danger lay in the strong, lurking current, a current that, if it didn't pull you down with it, would dash you into the rocks instead.

Taking a moment to steady myself, I saw that Dad was halfway into the cave already.

"Wait!" I said, afraid for him, but he powered on, confident in the knowledge the cleft was empty.

I followed, flicking on a small flashlight the owner of the Folly had provided in case of blackouts, which were common during the storms that battered the peninsula. It was attached to my belt with a carabiner, of which there seemed to be plenty at the Folly. They were very useful, and I felt rather adventurous with the torch dangling from my waist, as if I were an explorer with a loaded utility belt.

The cave was not big. More of a deep split in the cliff face, it had been abused and assaulted by the ocean so frequently I wondered if a large chunk of stone were about to fall upon our heads. I had seen it happen, first-hand, after the last storm: a section of the peninsula had given itself up to the sea as I had walked by, exposing a smaller fissure like this one, fissures that were old by human standards, but not by the standards of the water, the earth, the land, or the sky.

Inside this particular rupture in the granite, Dad and I found a deflated air bed spread out on the wet floor. It was covered in rancid bird droppings, a white paste that indicated no one had slept upon it for a while. Evidence of an uncomfortable, damp, transient life lay scattered about: empty food packets and tins already spotted with rust, a box of soggy matches, a few candles, long-extinguished, scraps of paper, the red apron that looked exactly like Mum's, but couldn't have been hers because that would have been absurd. It was crumpled and sodden with old blood that had not dried because of the moist nature of the cave, but I could still make out the letters HED CH, peeking out between folds of mildewing fabric. *Like Mum*, I thought. Mouldy and soft. This almost prompted a giggle out of me, although I couldn't have said why.

I aimed the torch beam at the cave walls, wanting to be sure there was no nook or cranny that the ruined body of the bald man could have been hiding in, waiting, folded up like a deck chair, crammed in like a snake under a rock, although I knew Dad was right, I knew we were alone.

As the torch light hit what should have been dark, water-stained stone, I gasped.

We may have been alone, but it seemed we were still part of a conversation I didn't want to have with a third party who refused to stop talking.

For the walls of the cave were covered with writing, smothered with scribbles, daubed with what I thought must have been paint, but was probably bird shit, or at least, I could only assume that, because what else would it be? It was yellowish-white, with dark streaks swirled in, almost like a toddler had gone haywire with a set of paints: it had that unhindered, slap-dash feel that characterised art made by children.

The message was simple, to the point. The same four digits, graffitied over and over and over again:

1976
   1976
   1976
   1976

. . .

The year before I was born.

"Dad?" I asked, feeling strange. The cave stank of damp and sea water and old blood and shit and something else I couldn't put my finger on. It was making me nauseous.

He didn't reply.

"Dad?" I repeated. "What happened in 1976?"

My father looked at the walls of the crevice and shook his head, just once, a terse gesture of denial. His shoulders were slumped. Any extra height he'd gained since leaving prison was lost again. In that moment he seemed defeated. It was the only word I could use to describe him. He'd given up. This made me both angry and scared. Angry, because it was increasingly evident he was hiding something significant from me. Scared, because I didn't know what the implications of his keeping secrets would have for us. For our future together.

"I'm hungry," he replied, avoiding eye contact. "The man isn't here. He's gone. Probably fell into the sea. Good riddance. Let's go back."

"What happened in 1976?" I asked again, suddenly needing to know. My voice came out like a child's: whining, thin, edged with entitlement. How dare he keep things from me. How *dare* he have secrets after everything I'd done for him. Everything I'd given up.

How *dare* he.

Finally, eye contact.

"Nothing," he lied.

His left eyelid twitched as he said it.

FOURTEEN

Dad used wooden stakes and heavy rope to make a rudimentary barrier across the part of the cliff where the niches led down to the cleft. He said it was to stop people falling down there by accident, but I suspected it was to keep me away from the cave graffiti. He knocked the makeshift fence up while I made lunch, watching him work through the kitchen porthole window, as had become habit.

Over sandwiches, I decided it was time to talk. Properly. I wanted answers. I wanted to be able to close my eyes without seeing the numbers 1976 on the insides of my eyelids. I lulled my father into a false sense of security, letting him eat half his meal, then I dropped the question.

"Dad. You can't avoid it forever. What happened in 1976?"

Dad dropped his sandwich, hands suddenly clumsy and uncooperative.

I tried again, rephrasing my question into a demand.

"Tell me what happened in 1976."

He gathered the soft bread and lettuce and ham back into a single entity, cramming it into his mouth to give him more time.

I waited.

I was long used to waiting.

I had waited years for him to come out, hadn't I?

I could wait a minute or two more.

He saw he wasn't going to wriggle out of it.

"Honestly," he replied, and I knew as soon as his mouth opened that he was going to lie to me again, "honestly, Morgan, I don't know. The only thing that happened to us in 1976 is that you were conceived. That's the only thing I can think of. And is that what you want to talk about, really? After everything we've seen?"

In a way, he was right. I knew it was absurd to focus on the year 1976 instead of the walking sack of skin and bones and blood that had spoken with the voice of my mother. A physical impossibility, an abomination of reality, and yet here I was, obsessed with 1976.

But I also knew it was important, the answer to this

question, and intrinsically linked to the other question that kept me awake each night.

Why had Mum come back to haunt us?

Dad, thinking the conversation now over, went back to his sandwich. His stubborn refusal to divulge the truth lit a fire in my belly that would not be easily put out.

What happened that year that Dad was so unwilling to tell me?

Fine, I thought. If he didn't want to share, I would extract something else from him.

He owed me, after all.

I didn't realise until that moment how much resentment I'd been storing up.

I changed tack.

"Dad," I said, carefully picking up the second half of my own sandwich and delicately peeling off the bread crust. I would eat it last, or maybe I would throw it out for the birds. I hadn't decided yet. It would depend on the conversation that was about to take place.

"What?" He looked harassed, suspicious. His eyes were hooded.

"Tell me what happened. In your words."

"When?"

I held his gaze. "The night Mum died."

Betrayal and hurt contorted his face.

I held firm.

"You offered to tell me a little while back. You offered it up, just like that, under the stars, said I could ask questions. So, now I'm asking questions."

Silence sat thick and heavy between us. I let it sit, refusing to back down.

Dad ran a hand across his lips, wiping away crumbs and sadness.

"But you heard it all in the trial, didn't you?" he said eventually. "Surely you don't want to go over it all again, not now."

His shift in attitude didn't make any sense. Why so keen to tell me then, but so reluctant now?

What had changed?

I had a feeling I knew.

"Tell me again. I want to hear it from your mouth." And I did, I really did. I didn't want to hear it from a lawyer. I didn't want to read it on a trashy news site. I didn't want to hear it in my own head, trying to make sense of the insensible.

I wanted it from him.

I wanted to know how and why my mother had died.

I wanted his testimony.

"Not now, Morgan. I'm tired. This isn't a good conversation for us to have right now."

"Yes, now, Dad. If not now, then never."

He smiled, half-heartedly. "Never sounds alright to me."

I shook my head, then slammed my hands on the table top. A glass of water too close to the edge of the table committed suicide, smashed on the floor. I thought again how strange it was that gravity had such a heavy pull here. Everything seemed to want to return to the earth, at speed, to destroy itself. Crockery. People. Maybe it was all those secrets, pulling everything down. That's why Jessica Harbourne had put aside her pen and flown from the tower top. Secrets like air beneath wings made of wax and stolen feathers. Eddies of deceit, carrying her to her doom.

Dad stared at me, then at the ruined glass. I was not usually a violent sort of person.

Not the sort of person to beat a bird to a pancake with a poker, I thought.

"Please," I said, my voice cracking. "I want to know. I've never asked you. Not once, not even when it happened."

"I know. You're a good girl, Morgan."

"*I'm forty fucking three years old!*" I roared, lobbing my plate, with the half-eaten sandwich on it, past his head. It struck the wall beyond, fractured in two, raining the meal I had carefully prepared onto the counter behind him: bread, filling, an apple, crackers, sliced carrots.

"Did you think I had no life of my own, Dad?" The words ripped out of me, my anger thundering along like a freight train with faulty brakes. "Or did you think I spent years campaigning for your release because there wasn't anything better to do? You know I had a boyfriend, right? When you were inside. I had a relationship, a good one, and it meant something. He wanted to marry me, you know. He...we..." I couldn't bring myself to share further than that, but my hand subconsciously drifted to my belly before I caught it, put it back on the table top again. "I put it all aside for you. *All* of it. I used all my money, all my time, all my energy. All my love. For you. To get you out. Doesn't that mean anything to you?"

"Of course it does." His face was like the hard granite rock of the cliffs nearby.

"Then tell me. You owe me, Dad. You fucking *owe* me an explanation. Not in front of a court. Not with your lawyer standing by. No jury. No judge. Just me. You owe me."

He gazed at me with fish-eyes, round and dead and shiny. I faced him, brimming with defiance and grief that had long since curdled and gone sour.

"Alright," he said eventually, in a cold, flat voice. "I'll tell you. What precisely do you want to know?"

I swallowed. My hands were shaking now.

Careful, Morgan, I told myself.

Do you really want this?

Do you really need another blow-by-blow account? You heard it all in court, like he said. How will this be different? Will it help you?

Yes. Yes, I did need it.

And yes, yes, it would.

"Tell me what happened that night." I would not ask again.

Dad leaned back in his chair, trained his eyes on the ceiling. He rested his hands across his own belly, and thought hard on the best way to start.

Then he said:

"Well, you know how your mother was sometimes."

And I had to fight hard not to reach over the table and slap him every which way but Sunday.

FIFTEEN

"Your mother could be difficult."

I held my tongue. My silence was more effective than any retort I might have had anyway.

Dad realised how that sounded, softened his phrasing.

"By that I mean...well, it wasn't always sunshine and sparkles, you know that. Marriage is hard work. We argued, every couple argues. That was one of those nights we'd...we'd had a row."

I knew this much. The official statement from Dad said they'd been going at each other about something, and Mum, in a fit of anger, had stormed off, slipped on the top of the stairs in her haste, and fallen to the bottom. The slippers she'd been wearing had taken a large portion of the blame. Slippers with a fur trim.

Slippers I'd bought her for Christmas.

The jury had not believed him, but I had. Mum rushed everywhere, clattering about at great speed, and she wasn't always careful as she went. She was routinely covered in bumps and cuts and scrapes. It hadn't come as a surprise to me that she'd fallen down the stairs, not really. Only a few weeks before, she'd walked into a cupboard, almost taken her eye out on a corner in the process. Six months prior to that, she'd slammed her finger in a drawer and broken it. She was always injuring herself, for as long as I could remember. The stairs had felt inevitable, almost.

And yet.

"Why did you wait to call the ambulance, Dad?" This was the main thing that had gone against him in his first trial. And I knew the answer, but I wanted to hear it from him. I wanted to see if I could make sense of it now some considerable time had passed.

"I was in shock," he parroted. Various lawyers over the years had taught him how. "I knew she was dead. That much blood...I went into shock. I couldn't think straight."

Again, I believed that much. Many others didn't, but I did. Dad had never been very good in an emergency, or with blood. Once, as a girl, I'd started my period while we were in the car on a daytrip. I had bled through my jeans, which had been white, of course. The mess was incredible, considering how little I'd actually leaked. Dad's face when he'd seen the spreading stain on my crotch was imprinted on my memory. He'd gone pale and still as a statue, unable to look at me for the rest of the day, even as I quietly cried with embarrassment in the car beside him. It was not that he was unsympathetic, I knew that. He just wasn't wired the same way I was, or Mum was. He wasn't a person who was comfortable with emotion, of any sort. He liked to laugh, sure, we all did. But he couldn't handle the other feelings, not really. They were beyond the scope of his chemistry.

So yes, I had found it a realistic notion that, confronted with such a horrific scene, he had simply shut down. I'd always envisaged him sitting at the top of the stairs for hours, a grim, sad gargoyle above a dead body, head in hands, staring but not seeing, until I'd come home, found them both thus.

He proceeded to shatter that image with a single sentence I'd never heard before.

"I knew she was dead. There was no point calling anyone. The state she was in...her head all twisted like that...I could see she was dead."

I sighed. "I'm sorry, Dad."

"So, I had a drink instead."

I froze.

What?

"You had...a drink?"

He nodded, speaking now as if in a trance. "I saw her, at the bottom of the stairs. I knew she was gone. Her neck, like I said. And I saw her brains. On the rug in the hallway. Looked like porridge, they did. Nobody could survive that. And if she had survived...there wouldn't have been much of her left, would there. She wouldn't have wanted that. A ventilator. Everyone hanging around her waiting for her to wake up. She wasn't that sort of person. Not a vegetable, not my wife. So I came down the stairs, carefully, trying not to stand in any blood or stuff. I stepped over her and went to the living room and made a whisky and soda."

"You made a drink while...she lay there?"

"Whisky and soda."

"Instead of calling the ambulance?"

Why hadn't this come out in either of the trials? Why had he never, in all the times I had asked him about it, told me this?

What was happening?

Was he lying again? Did he have it all mixed up?

Or had he held this back from me until now because...

Because it was incriminating?

He let his gaze come back down off the ceiling, so I

was no longer staring at the underside of his chin. His eyes when they met mine were dark, and honest.

"I couldn't find the spoon we use normally, to mix drinks. Had to use my finger instead. Round and around, like this." He made a downwards spiral motion with his left index finger, and I was reminded chillingly of the bald man twirling imaginary hair. "Wiped the blood off it first, of course."

I swallowed. The world dipped and rocked and rose and crested around me, like the floor had become the sea, and I was a tiny, fragile boat on the waves.

"Why...?" I had to clear my throat of phlegm to let the words out. "Why was there blood on your hands, Dad?"

He was done talking, I could see. He'd run out of steam, and words, and honesty.

"Dad? Why was there blood on your hands?"

He didn't answer.

"What were you arguing about, you and Mum?"

Still no reply.

"Dad? Please." I whispered it, for I was out of fight.

"I can't really remember," he mumbled, then picked up the remnants of his sandwich and began to eat as if nothing had happened.

I stood abruptly. My head spun as if I was drunk.

"I need to start on dinner." I didn't know what else to say.

"We haven't finished lunch yet," my father replied.

"Then I'm going for a walk!"

I scrambled from the room as fast as I could, thundering down the iron steps too quickly for comfort, gripping the handrail so tightly I thought I might yank it from the wall brackets.

"All that stuff about believing me was bullshit then?" Dad shouted after me. "Despite everything you said?"

I chose not to reply.

It was safer not to.

Sixteen

I walked, just like I said I would, taking the path to the edge of the cliffs, around the hook, then back into the woods behind the Folly. My head still spun.

He had made himself a drink?

I tried to remember if I'd seen a whisky glass anywhere when I'd come home. Then I realised how useless it was to attempt a recall of something so small, so seemingly insignificant. All my attention had been focused on Mum lying at the foot of the stairs. Dad had been sitting at the top, staring at me in horror as I'd opened the front door. Had he been holding the glass, like he said? I just couldn't say.

I attempted once more to make sense of the sequence of events.

So he'd gone downstairs, stepped over Mum's body, made himself a drink, and then, what?

Gone back up to wait for me?

None of this means he is guilty, I tried to tell myself.

It just means he behaved erratically.

And yet I felt more anguish now than I had during Dad's first trial.

I thought we were done with all of this, I thought we were done analysing every tiny movement and second of that night.

I thought we were moving on.

I thought...

And what was it about 1976?

What was it my mother was trying to tell me?

Had it really been my mother speaking to me from another body?

Or a deranged person from her past trying to make a statement?

I would have believed that, had I not heard the bald man speak with her voice.

I would have believed that, had I not seen the bald man stand up and walk off with a broken leg and smashed ribs and his innards spilling out after falling from a huge height.

Had that, in fact, even happened, though?

There was no evidence for me to refer to, was there?

Dad had seen it, too.

Hadn't he?

All remains of the stranger had been washed away until there was only bleached grass left to tell the tale.

No, the only thing left was my own, unreliable memory.

Unreliable. Because I had been under a lot of stress, a lot of strain, after all.

Maybe I'd imagined the whole thing.

Maybe it had been a nightmare, and I was still asleep.

Maybe I'd had a temporary episode of delusion, a hallucination.

I stopped dead in my tracks as I realised what I was doing.

I was trying to reason myself out of something I had witnessed, something I had seen with my own two eyes.

I lacked evidence, sure.

But I had seen the man walk away.

I had *seen* it.

Just like I had seen Mum's body.

What was I trying to tell myself?

What connection was I trying to make?

Lack of evidence.

Lack.

Of.

Evidence.

Dad's face came to mind. Harrowed, haunted. Sitting at the top of the stairs.

Swirling a bloodied finger in a glass of whisky and soda.

Wiped the blood off it first, of course.

A lack of evidence didn't mean something didn't happen.

In a court of law, that was one thing.

In the court of life...

I wondered.

Dad was free now.

Should Dad be free now?

I had no evidence that he'd done anything to Mum.

No evidence.

That was why, eventually, when he was retried, he was released. He'd been wrongly convicted on a lack of concrete evidence. Nothing forensic. Nothing circumstantial. Nothing by which, reasonably, a man should be sequestered, should have his freedom taken from him.

And yet.

And.

Yet.

I'd been so convinced of his innocence.

I'd fought for him from the very moment he was arrested and charged with Mum's death. A death that had eventually, after many years of injustice, been declared accidental.

But was it?

An accident?

How could I be so sure?

There was no evidence to tie Dad to her death!

But there was no evidence to *clear* him of it either.

In that respect, he was like a ghost. I did not believe in ghosts, or had not, until we'd moved to the Folly. Because there had been no concrete, scientifically accepted evidence, in my opinion or experience, that ghosts ever existed.

But there had never been any concrete, scientific evidence that they *didn't*.

I was out of my depth, swimming in uncertainty as surely as if I had fallen into the ocean.

Light-headed, overwhelmed, I knew I needed to sit down before I stumbled and fell on the path.

I found a tree, put it against my back, sinking slowly down to the earth. Overhead, branches interlaced and made patterns against the blue. I sat, drawing my knees up to my chest, sinking my head into them, trying to find stability. Trying to find equilibrium.

Had I made a mistake?

Had I fought for the wrong person all these years?

Had I given up so much of my life for the wrong cause?

What happened in 1976?

I started to cry, unable to think anymore. My head. My poor head.

I cried, feeling as if my heart were breaking all over again, and the trees went on swaying above me, were they comforting me with their branches softly chattering?

If they were, I could not accept the...

A hand emerged from the undergrowth nearby and grabbed my ankle, squeezing it tight.

I screamed, kicking out.

The decaying, sunken face of the bald man leered up at me from a patch of nettles and ferns.

Found him.

His lips had been eaten away by something, rats maybe, foxes. His eyes were clouded and milky as rough sea surf. Woodlice gathered in the hollows of his nostrils. His tongue hung loose and ragged and almost dislocated from a shattered jaw, a jaw which worked regardless. A single, sibilant word leaked out of the man's slack mouth like discharge, nearly unintelligible, but I had seen the cave walls, so translating his dead language was easy.

"1976," my mother's voice said, and I ripped the rotting hand from my body and scrambled upright, almost letting go of my bladder.

"LEAVE ME ALONE!" I screamed, but I found I was screaming at nothing, for there was nothing there, no stranger, no hand grasping for me, only undergrowth and brambles and nettles. I was alone, and maybe that was the problem.

I was falling apart, and there was no one to witness me.

I bolted through the woods, running away from my own madness and nightmares until I reached the Folly front door, whereupon I slammed it, bolted it, locked it, and sat with my back to it, crying once more.

Dad did not come find me this time. I was fine with that. I didn't want him near me.

Later, though, I heard him crying too, in his room.

The Folly drank the tears, as was its way.

SEVENTEEN

The pubs reopened two months later. Slowly, and not with the bang of celebration everyone expected. People were tired, and emerged from lockdown blinking, as Dad had emerged from prison that day.

I decided to take him for Sunday lunch in Mousehole. I had to book a table first. It took me three days to get a slot, which was timed, limited to an hour and a half only, but that was okay. We didn't need that long. Just long enough to make an effort.

I had to try. Even if my heart was not fully in it.

Our relationship had deteriorated significantly since Dad told me about the night Mum died. I had kept largely to myself in the weeks that followed, but I noticed Dad acting more and more strangely. Sleep seemed to elude him entirely, and I knew he was getting maybe two, three hours, tops, a night. Worse than when he'd been in prison. He was not the only one. I didn't sleep much either. Whenever I closed my eyes, I felt a rotting hand wrap itself around my ankle. When that image dissolved, it was invariably replaced with the broken bird, or the shambling form of the bald man limping away, or my mother's brains on the rug. I wished fervently that I had access to sleeping pills, or even alcohol, but I had deliberately kept the Folly dry of both medication and booze, for what I had thought were the best of reasons.

Sometimes, Dad would take walks in the dark, and I would hear him go, tip-tapping down the iron stairs, and I would wonder if he had a torch with him, or if he would tumble off the cliffs by mistake and I would have to go out and find his body the next morning, because that seemed to be my fate: stumbling, unprepared, across the dead.

His insomnia, and mine, made us groggy and recalcitrant during the day. His appetite waned, which upset me more than anything because it felt like a giant step backward, for both of us. But equally, I had stopped making such an effort with the food, and he could tell. My own fatigue coloured everything I did: cooking, cleaning, tidying, the pleasure I took in my walks around the cliffs. It felt as if the hue had been sucked out of the world, and I was a smudge on a blurred painting, all greys and ochres and indistinct, fuzzy smears.

The times Dad was sluggish were contrasted with periods of almost manic energy from him, which would occur without warning. During these phases he would clean windows or rearrange cupboards or scrub the bathtub or dust and polish surfaces with the frenetic vigour of a man with nothing else better to do. The rest of the time, he patrolled the grounds with the iron poker, which I could no longer bear to look at.

Once, I heard strange, choked noises coming from his room and charged up there, thinking again that he was taking steps to end things. When I slammed his door open, I found him half naked at the end of his bed, trousers in a puddle around his ankles, hand working furiously up and down around himself, eyes closed in a painful grimace, and I backed away so fast I nearly ended up the same way as Mum. I had never thought of Dad in that way until that moment, although I knew my parents were as human as I was, and bursting in on him like he was a teenager caught in the act was cripplingly embarrassing and degrading, for both of us.

After that, our strained silences were even more laden with awkwardness, and we stopped eating meals together completely. I would make food when I was hungry and save him some, and he would eat it when he felt like it, or he wouldn't, which was the case more often than not.

And all the while I kept thinking: *What happened in 1976?*

When the world slowly opened up again, I saw it as an opportunity to start things fresh with Dad. It didn't really matter if I believed him about Mum's death, I had come to realise, with effort. We lived together. This was our new life, our only reality. I had no money to move anywhere else, and neither did he. And I loved him still, or at least, the little girl in me did. He was my father. I had nowhere else to go, very little in the way of options.

So I booked a table in the nice, quaint old pub I'd found a leaflet for, thinking that, in a different, busier setting, perhaps we could move on, develop trust once more. I was willing to try.

Make the best of it, as Mum would say, and I tried. We could just about afford it with the money we hadn't spent on groceries and the rent that the landowner was covering. I also had a tiny pot of savings held back, a hundred quid, no more, for just this sort of thing. And some coupons, cut from a tourist pamphlet I'd found in a drawer in the Folly.

We drove in silence to Mousehole—aptly named, for everything was on a scale so cramped and narrow we felt like rodents running through tunnels as I pulled the car down several tiny one-way streets. We nudged our way along until we reached the busy harbourside car park and squeezed into a spot between a camper van and a touring bike. It was strange seeing public spaces and amenities in a crowded state again. There were people milling about everywhere. I had been so used to the desolate air of a pandemic that I was more than a little overwhelmed with all the families and couples out and about, and even though we all knew things weren't back to normal completely, they were just normal enough that we could start to recover, slowly, suspiciously, none of us quite believing the state of freedom would last.

The pub was on the waterfront, with heavy casement-style windows that overlooked the harbour. They were open to let air circulate better inside the low-ceilinged, beam-heavy inn that was truly from a bygone era. Easily three or four hundred years old, the floors were wonky, the walls leaned in and out and all over the place, and the light was low, atmospheric, to the point of reminding me of the cave in the cliff near the Folly. The food smelled good: solid fried fare, wholesome, filling, simple, not particularly healthy.

Dad ordered a half pint of Tribute and I ordered a tonic water, which came in a fancy bowl-glass with lemon and ice, the generous garnish there to compensate for the teetotal nature of the drink. We studied the menu diligently, although we both knew what we wanted—I would have fish and chips, and dad would order the ploughman's. We had been ordering the same things ever since I was old enough to be taken to the pub.

Mum would always have lamb, if it was available.

I saw lamb on the menu, and took a huge gulp of my tonic.

The waitress came over, which took some getting used to. In pubs like this, I usually had to elbow my way to the front of the bar to place an order, but again, the pandemic had changed all that. Table service was preferable, actually, and eminently less stressful. I never had been very good at getting anyone's attention.

"Ready to order?" she asked in a bright, rather false tone that was muffled by a surgical facemask. Her eyes, heavily rimmed with liner, twinkled over the top of the blue synthetic covering. I wondered, as I always did, if the eyes were lying above the thin material. If below, her mouth was actually arranged in a thin, bored line, not a smile. I wanted so fervently for the era of masks to be over, for they made me anxious, but I understood their necessity.

It just felt easier to trust someone when you could see their whole face, was all.

"Fish and chips, please," I said politely.

She wrote it down on her small notepad.

"And for you?" she asked, looking at Dad, and then did a very obvious double-take.

My heart sank.

Her eyes narrowed.

She recognised him.

I could tell, not just by the eyes, but by the way her body language changed. She stiffened, closed herself up. Drew the shutters down.

Dad registered the change in her, too. Took it in his stride.

"I'll have the lamb, please," he said.

I stared at him. I suddenly felt sick.

He handed the waitress the menu, and she took it silently. I hoped nobody would spit in Dad's food while it was being prepared.

"What are you doing?" I murmured in confusion as the waitress left, throwing a pointed look back over her shoulder as she went.

"I like lamb," he replied simply.

He knew exactly what he was doing, I realised.

He pushed his chair back. "I need a piss," he said, by way of explanation, and I was left staring out the window at the sea, wondering what had become of my life.

While he was away, the waitress came back with knives and forks and napkins.

She placed a bundle of cutlery carefully on the table next to me. Cleared her throat.

Here we go, I thought.

It was a wonder we'd been able to avoid it as long as we had.

This was why we'd moved out to the Folly.

"It took me a while," she said, "but I recognised you both in the end."

My heart sank even further. "I doubt it," I tried, but my face was not a convincing display.

She pulled her mask down below her chin, and smiled. It was a pretty smile, not a mouth-lie, but condescending. She was young, bright, and curious. I found it intimidating.

"Oh, I definitely figured it out. And it's none of my business but...are you sure you're safe with him, sweetheart?"

I stared at her, galled at her overfamiliarity. The temerity of calling a woman twice her age *sweetheart* pricked at me more than anything else.

"What do you mean?"

But I knew very well what she meant.

She crouched down so we could share an eye-line.

"Look, I understand," she said, and her tone could not have been more patronising if she'd tried. "We all love our daddies. But he killed your mum, didn't he? Are you sure you should be living alone with him all the way out there in that tower?"

Numb, I worked my suddenly dry mouth.

"How did you know we...?"

"Oh, the whole town knows there's a convict out on the peninsula with his daughter. Can't keep secrets around here, not with how small the place is. Everyone knows everyone in the West Country, don't they?"

And there was me thinking we had escaped all of this. I had been living in ignorance, it turned out, about a whole lot of things.

She leaned in conspiratorially.

"I mean...there are a *lot* of stairs in that place," she continued, her eyes wide with dramatic intent.

I surged up from the table and stalked quickly to the toilets, where I just about avoided being sick. I passed Dad on the way, but didn't stop to talk. He watched me pass with eyes filled with concern, and yet there was something else there, too, something harder. Defiance? I didn't have the mental fortitude to try to figure it out.

I splashed my face with cold water, avoiding my reflection in the bathroom mirror as usual.

Common sense dictated that we leave the pub after that, avoid further scrutiny, but I had come prepared to pay for lunch, so we sat there in strained silence until Dad motioned to the waitress, holding up his empty pint glass to order another Tribute.

When it arrived, it was flat, the end of the barrel, and there looked to be something strange floating in it.

"I wouldn't drink that, if I were you," I muttered.

He looked me dead in the eye, and drank his pint down in one long, laborious go, spit and all.

Then he wiped his face with the back of his hand and ordered another.

The food arrived, and we ate it, even though every bite tasted like hot lead, and I felt the eyes of the bar staff on me the whole time. I knew they would not even wait for us to leave before gossiping about us. As I raised my head occasionally from my meal, I saw the patrons of the pub throwing glances our way too, or rather, dirty looks at Dad and pitying looks at me, and I wanted to scream at them, "Don't you know he was found innocent in a court of law?" But I had tried that once before, I had tried to make people see, and failed, and the only thing that had come back to me had been talk of technicalities and, honestly, what was the point? Again, who was I even trying to convince?

Them, or myself?

No, I had to stop this. I had to, for my own sanity. Dad was found innocent by a court of law. Dad had loved Mum, and me, and that had been real, and it still was real, and no amount of public discourse was going to change that. Whisky, or no whisky.

I went again to the toilets for one last splash of cold water on my face before we drove back to the Folly. I was in a calmer state after eating. The worst was behind us now, this outing almost over, so I walked more slowly, took in more details.

On the wall next to the lavatories, I spotted a series of faded glossy photographs. I'd rushed past them before, but this time I was more observant. The photographs largely displayed the ubiquitous shots of the cast and crew of *The Wailing Pillar* movie, as promised by the Folly's owner. The biggest frame showed the infamous author of the novel standing next to the lead actress who was smiling in crinoline, a cigarette dangling from one hand. The Folly itself loomed in the background. There were other pictures, too, local scenes. Local people. One of them held my eye, and fired something in my brain, meaning that even though I initially walked past, I felt compelled to backstep, get a better look.

Large, skewed in its frame, and still colourful, in a tired way, it was a photograph of a group of men, fishermen, I realised, posing in front of one of the beached fishing boats in the harbour.

It was the name of the boat that had brought me up short: *MORGAN* was painted onto her in ornate black lettering.

In the middle of the group, a familiar bald-headed man. He stood the tallest of those assembled, arms slung around two friends. He was wearing a thick cable-knit sweater and long yellow wellington boots. I almost didn't recognise him, for a cap was slung across his usually bare head.

The waitress passed me as I stared at the picture. I grabbed her arm gently as she squeezed by in the narrow corridor. She reacted warily, pulling back, expecting some retaliation for her cheek earlier, perhaps, but my attention was on the photograph.

"Who's that?" I asked. Something about my face made it obvious that a lot hinged on her reply.

"Oh, that's Bill," she said. "Bill Southgood. One of the locals. He's usually in here on a weekend. Come to think of it, we haven't seen him since we re-opened. Which is surprising, because he's usually in here more than he's at home, or at least he was before all the nonsense with the pandemic. Loves a drink, does Bill. Most of our fishermen do." She squinted at him, and then at me.

"You look like him, you know," she said, and she was right. I hadn't seen it before, but she was right. If you had placed this photograph next to a recent one of me, which didn't exist, the similarities would be clear. Especially with my short hair. The shape of our head, most noticeably. The ears.

The likeness was suddenly, immediately obvious.

More obvious than it has ever been with Dad, I thought.

I'd always just assumed that perhaps women looked more like their mothers as they grew older but...

Was that true?

The waitress carefully extricated herself from my grasp and disappeared into the shadows of the pub.

The stranger looked happy in the picture. Relaxed. Natural, surrounded by kith and kin.

Nothing like the deranged puppet I'd seen leap from the top of the Folly.

Did I have to feel guilty about his death, too now?

Was he even really dead?

If so, where was his body?

And what happened in 1976?

Eighteen

Dad got sick four days later.

It started with a low-grade fever, a headache, a slight cough. Within days, he was bed-ridden, ashen-faced despite his fever, and his cough became so severe that sometimes, as I lay there listening to him hacking away in the small hours of the morning, I was sure I could feel the walls of the Folly vibrate with his sickness. More weight fell away from him, and I had to start changing his sheets daily because he sweated into them so much, even with the windows wide open and the fresh sea air swirling freely through the Folly. It felt wrong for the weather outside to be so beautiful and breezy while he was festering inside, deteriorating, but it made for a quick dry once I had washed the sheets, which was something.

On day five, I was sufficiently worried enough to call the doctor. I didn't feel as if an ambulance was needed, not yet, but I wasn't far from it. I knew the local surgery was likely to be overwhelmed, but I rang and I rang and I waited on hold and I pressed the requisite keys until finally, after what felt like aeons, I managed to speak to someone and explain our predicament.

The doctor came, despite all my doubts that anyone would be able to. Perhaps our circumstances were unique enough that we bucked the trend of not qualifying for a home visit. Perhaps the doctor knew enough about us that he simply wanted to ogle and have a story to go home to his wife with: "You know that wife-killer? Yes, well, I treated him today." "Oh, did you, darling? How thrilling!"

I put these mean thoughts to one side the second I saw him. The doc arrived in a bundle of protective masks and gloves and a clear plastic visor and I felt for him as he walked in: he looked exhausted, his cheeks raw from the facemask. I could see where it had rubbed a sore red line under his tired eyes and across the bridge of his nose and cheekbones.

He was quiet as he checked Dad's temperature, listened to his chest, felt his glands, did other things I didn't understand. I let him get on with it, knowing how to step back and allow someone to do their job, no matter how hard, no matter how involved I wanted to be. It had been the same with Dad's lawyers over the years. I had learned how to put my trust in them, despite how hard that had been.

Ten minutes later, the doc started to make preparations to leave. I escorted him down the stairs, waiting until we were at the bottom until I asked the question I most needed an answer to.

"Will he be okay?"

I realised, as I said it, that I was not ready to lose him again. Not after everything. Not now. No matter what he had done. He was my dad. He was my family, perhaps the only remaining member of it that I had any sort of relationship with.

I couldn't be left alone, not again.

The doctor looked me in the eye, serious, kind.

"In all honesty, he should probably be in the hospital. He is seriously sick, but you know that." His voice carried the same tone of defeat I'd seen and heard in Dad many times before.

"Should I call the ambulance?"

The doctor sighed. It was clear he didn't really know what to do, and that realisation tore at me.

"It's a difficult one. I would say he's perhaps too fragile to move from here easily. Getting him down those stairs...getting an ambulance close to the tower..."

He shook his head, and I knew he was right. "And right now, hospitals..." He shook his head again. I had never seen such a weary individual. It was a stark reminder that, no matter how bad I thought my own life was, someone else's was always worse.

"It's probably safer for him here. His breathing isn't as bad as it could be, there is some fluid on his lungs, but I can treat that with the new antivirals we are now getting. Keep him propped up with pillows, if you can. I can come back tomorrow. If not me, then the district nurse can, providing she doesn't drop out sick. Half the country is out of action, you know. Things are opening up, but...we're still fighting the fight. The virus doesn't stop just because the pubs are all open." He let out a bitter, frustrated laugh.

"What else can I do? To make him more comfortable?"

"Keep him hydrated, and as well fed as you can. He can't taste or smell anything, and he's nauseous, so he won't want to eat, but he has to. He needs fluid above all else. And you can give him painkillers. Check his temperature regularly and control it with flu medicine. Keep him propped upright, too. Did I say that already?"

"You did, but it's okay."

The doctor looked up at the tower. "I've never liked this building, you know. Too many sad things happened here. The locals have a ghoulish obsession with it."

I stared at him, not seeing the relevance but not wanting to give him a hard time about it. He was fragile, we all were.

"I appreciate you coming out. I know it's not how things are usually done."

He waved a hand. "It was good to get out of the surgery for a while, quite honestly. I'll prescribe your father some multivitamins, too, some industrial strength ones. He's not looking too healthy."

"I tried. After prison...I tried, but he just lost interest in food."

"I'm not suggesting it was your fault. You can't solve years and years of malnutrition in a few months, it takes time. You're doing the best you can."

"Thanks." I hadn't realised how fervently I'd needed to hear that.

"Beyond that, keep a close eye on his breathing. Call an ambulance if it looks as if he can't get any air in or if his fever worsens. This is a waiting game, I'm afraid. He'll either come out of it, or he won't. I know that's not what you want to hear."

"At this point," I said, staring off into the sea, "I have heard so many things, I hardly know what I want anymore."

The doctor was too beaten down to ask me what I meant. He simply squeezed my shoulder and promised to try to return the next day.

Why couldn't he have been my dad instead? I thought as I watched him leave.

Nineteen

"I might die tomorrow," Dad said in the middle of the night. His face was grey and thin, and he was wheezing worse than he had when he'd eventually woken up that morning.

I tried to feed him a sip of water, but he turned his head. This prompted me to snap at him, when I knew I should be gentle, but I could no longer help myself. There was only so much one person could handle and remain calm, and kind. He would have to accept me at my most impatient, for I was tired, and worried, and out of ideas.

"Jesus, Dad. You're not going to die," I said with more conviction than I felt. "You just have a virus. Plenty of people have gotten through it."

"Plenty of people have died, too," he replied, and I

couldn't argue with that. So instead, I held his hand and we sat in silence for a while. Outside, a seagull cried into the dark. Didn't they sleep like us? Evidently not.

I envied the bird, free to wheel and soar.

More silence, broken only by the perpetual crackle of fluid building in Dad's lungs.

Don't die, I thought helplessly. *Not like this. We'd only just gotten started. We can try again. And again. And as many times as we need to get it right.*

Don't die, Daddy.

"You asked me what happened in 1976," Dad said suddenly.

I froze in the act of surreptitiously wiping tears away with my free hand. I wanted to know, of course I did.

But now, like this?

It felt cruel to expect the truth from him as he lay there fighting such an insidious sickness.

Even with the whiskey and soda?

Yes, even with the whiskey and soda, I thought.

"Not now, Dad," I said out loud, feeling suddenly humbled.

But Dad insisted. Maybe the thought of dying had unlocked that sunken treasure chest in his heart, the one that held the truth. He didn't want to drown with it buried down deep in the depths, secrets and sins, tarnished gold.

"We always wanted you to think you were born

from love, not...not what happened," he said, and his hand felt cold, while his face radiated heat.

My stomach lurched. I remained quiet, because an interruption right now was not in my power.

"There was so much shame, you see. She felt so torn."

More silence, and painful, wet breaths.

Eventually, just when I thought he had dropped back into sleep, he repeated the word.

"Shame."

"Shame?"

"Because what happened...you have to understand, what happened to her was not her fault. Not really. She was young. Easily led. But back then, a girl couldn't come out of something like that well. They would have made it all her fault, and none of his."

I don't think I want to hear this, after all, I thought. *Not out loud. It can't be taken back once it's said out loud.* But the protestations were trapped inside my head, unable to break out. Like the inmates of a prison, all my power was walled in, bricked up. It was Dad's turn now, not mine. He was on the outside, and I was on the inside. Was the gravity stronger there or here?

Funny how life works, I thought.

"Fault?" I whispered.

"Her fault. When it wasn't. It was his."

He lifted his head then, and stared at me, tears starting to gather in his eyes.

"We wanted you to know you came from love, not a nasty fumble in the back of a car. You came from love. The second I held you in my arms, I knew I'd do anything to show you that you were loved. Anything."

The enormity of what he was saying began to sink in.

"He didn't deserve you. I was your dad. Not him."

A picture on a pub wall.

A boat named Morgan.

You look like him, you know.

Ask him what happened in 1976.

You were named for the sea.

But who had named me?

Mum?

Or the stranger?

I felt hollow, as if every part of me had been scooped out with a sharp-edged spoon.

"And then, that night...he came back."

I could barely see for the tears that had fuzzed my vision.

"He did?"

"All those years later. He just wandered into our lives, said he wanted to be your dad again. He had no right. NO RIGHT!" He tried to shout it, and I realised he was burning up now, his fever had escalated. How much of what he was saying could I trust?

"Shh, Dad!" I tried to settle him back on the pillow but he fought me, staring at something over my shoulder, ranting, furious.

"You came back. WHY DID YOU COME BACK?"

A noise behind me made me realise that he wasn't ranting into thin air.

He wasn't delusional with fever.

He was shouting *at* someone.

The Folly had been breached once more.

"Because she had a right to know, Owen," the bald man replied softly in Mum's voice.

I turned slowly to see him leaning against the doorframe of Dad's bedroom. His leg was in filthy, self-administered bandages with a crude splint lashed to it with fishing twine. Old blood leaked through the dingy wrapping, and I was in awe of how he had survived infection. He did not look as if he was fighting pain, or sepsis, or anything. His skin tone was ruddy, healthy, almost, the opposite of Dad's.

I no longer questioned how he had gotten in. It was a pointless question that meant nothing in the scheme of what was unfolding.

"Get out," I whispered, but I knew he wouldn't.

The strange man—my father—smiled, and for the

first time since he had come into our lives, uninvited, it was not a smile born of malice or duplicity or revenge. He turned it on like a lighthouse beam, and his hard, seagull-stare softened. And, now that I knew him for who he was, I could see myself in that smile, and it should have brought me some peace, some closure, but I felt sick, sick to my very soul. *No sea legs on her, she can't be my real daughter*—because what right did he have to smile at me that way? He wasn't my father, he wasn't anything, he was as inconsequential as the bleached grass beneath the foot of the Folly, he was part of the scenery and nothing more. Except that wasn't true, was it? That wasn't true.

Is that why you're upset, Morgan?

I knew it wasn't.

I knew the real reason I was upset.

I was upset because I finally knew what Mum and Dad had been arguing about the night she fell.

I was upset because, although there was a distinct lack of evidence surrounding Dad's guilt or assumed innocence, I had, without wanting it, definitive proof of something else.

I had proof that he could, in fact, have done it. Pushed her.

Because now, I had a motive.

Dad had given me a solid, good, old-fashioned motive for my mother's murder.

I was not his child. Not by birth. Not by blood.

He had been trying to keep secrets from me.

I pulled my hand out of his cold, clammy grasp.

The stranger spoke again. What was his name? I fought hard to remember what the barmaid had said.

Bill. Bill Southgood.

"I came back because I wanted my daughter to know me," he said in his own voice, all traces of my Mum now gone.

And I had a horrible feeling he meant it. I had a horrible feeling he was full of remorse, in a way, for missing my life, and that he had, in his own manner, perhaps loved my mother, even if only briefly, or at least thought he had loved her, in the moment, perhaps, and now he thought he loved me, too, even though he had never bounced me upon his knee, paid for my driving lessons, changed me as a baby or carried me sleeping in his arms, played badminton in the garden with me in the long summer evenings that never seemed to end, carved trinkets for me out of wood, or picked berries with me in the frost-tipped mornings of November, my favourite month. He had never wiped my tears away with the heel of his hand, smiled in a graduation photograph, waded into a pond to rescue a teddy bear I had let go of at just the wrong time. He had never done any of those things because he was not my Dad.

Inside the walls of one terrible, cold second in time, I

lost my father and gained a new one. A father I didn't want.

And it felt as if I were being ripped in half, right down the middle, like a sheet of paper held fast in two hands.

"I think you should leave," I told Southgood, feeling my resilience shred into tiny pieces and float off on a strong coastal breeze. "I think you should leave us both alone in peace."

The rejection stung him more than I thought it would. I saw it play out on his face in stages—disbelief, then wry denial, then anger—and I wondered if my mother had said no to him in exactly the same way, I wondered if his face had looked like this just before he had decided her refusal wasn't valid. His features twisted and I hoped, fervently, that I would never, ever look like that. I hoped genetics would fail me, because I saw only a monster, not a man. I saw nothing worth redeeming, even though Dad had always been the one to tell me that everyone, even the lowest, most hateful person, had something good hiding in them, some quality. It was hard to believe that, looking at the stranger; it was hard to believe in anything much anymore. I'd been stripped of all my certainties, and felt horribly naked.

Suddenly, a swim in the ocean felt like a good idea.

"I'm not going to leave," Southgood said in a matter-of-fact-voice. He swayed a little: the injured leg was giving him more grief than he was willing to let on. "I have a right. You're blood. I deserve a chance. I was never given a chance. He kept me away from you. I wanted...I just wanted a chance."

I did not hear this. Instead, I heard "Waterloo" playing faintly from the radio in the kitchen. I heard different words from my new father's lips:

"I'm going to haunt your every step," he said in my mind, his lips livid with rot, Mum's voice seeping out through the cracks in his dirty teeth. "Until you can no longer sleep at night. You'll never know where I am, or when I will show up. I'll make sure of that."

"We will call the police," I tried to say, but I felt too disconnected to finish the sentence: *We can get a restraining order, there are things we can do.*

Looking down at my dad, hoping, a child once again, that he could provide me with some guidance, or reassurance, I saw he had taken a turn for the worse. His chest fluttered in and out, struggling for any small morsel of air. He was dying, I realised, in shock.

That quickly?

He had been fine a few days ago!

Wait.

What?

Was this real?

Was any of it real?

I was holding a small cushion in my hands suddenly.

Had that been there for long?

There was spittle on it.

Dad's chest fell.

It didn't rise again.

His hand went slack.

A final, pained rattle filled the air.

"Dad?" I whispered, my eyes burning with his death.

And in my mind, the fictional conversation continued with my new Dad.

"Think they are going to take the word of a convicted murderer?" the bald man said, eyes ablaze with mockery. "A man who killed his wife and got away with it? I don't."

"It was an accident," I murmured, rising slowly from Dad's bedside. My head was pounding.

"What? Morgan? What...? Morgan!"

He no longer frightened me. I had nothing left, and that made me bold.

So I walked right up to him and pushed him, hard, placing both hands on his chest and shoving with all my might.

He tumbled back, and although it should have been louder, the sound of his body hitting every single step on the way down the spiral staircase, it wasn't. For some reason, all I could hear instead was the cry of a gull, wheeling in the sky outside, and beyond that, the call of the ocean, which told me to come.

TWENTY

I found myself on the tip of the peninsula, stumbling like a zombie, trying to put the Folly, my failed home, behind me. The wind was picking up, and a storm played with the light out on the horizon. I knew from experience that it would not take long to move inland, storms never did. For now, early stars still shone valiantly, but soon all would be cold, and wet, like my heart.

In my head, my two dead fathers argued with each other.

"Lose your temper with her, did you?"

"Shut the fuck up."

"She tell you she was considering coming clean, did she?"

"Shut the fuck up before I make you."

"She was going to tell her about me, you know. She agreed with me. Said it was time I was part of Morgan's life, that it was high time she knew the truth, she said it wasn't fair to keep secrets. She said you couldn't love someone properly and keep secrets. Was she right?"

"Dad?" I cried the word out into the night, but no one replied. I felt very cold, and very confused. What was happening to me?

"She told you she was going to come clean, and you lost your temper, didn't you?"

"Dad?"

"It wasn't an accident, was it?"

"Leave him alone, please. Please leave us both alone!"

"It wasn't diminished responsibility at all, was it? There was no mistrial. No miscarriage of justice."

"Please stop, both of you."

"You bottled it up for years, didn't you? Felt emasculated, didn't you? You never had a baby of your own, did you? She chose my baby over your feelings, didn't she?"

"I loved her! Her business does not belong in your mouth!"

"Got angry, didn't you?" Was this the stranger speaking now, or me?

"You supported her for all those years, you raised her child, you put aside any hopes of a family of your own, and what did she do in the end? Turned around and betrayed you. But that's what women do, Owen. I told you that years ago. You can't trust them. You can never trust them."

"Dad?"

"He isn't your dad, sweetheart. I am. And guess what? He killed your mother."

"Dad?"

"Ask him."

"Shut up."

"Ask him."

"Shut up"

"I SAID FUCKING ASK HIM!" The words were lifted on a raw, wet gust of wind that battered me out of nowhere. The sea, my constant companion, began to churn. The storm had blown in, as storms do. Swift, furious. White horses charging.

"I'm sorry," my real Dad's voice said. "I'm so sorry."

But was that him?

Or was it the other one?

Then I was teetering just shy of the edge of the cliff, a few paces from the wet, heaving body of water, staring down into a stirring void laced with froth.

"You tried your best for me. That's more than any man could have asked, Morgan."

The seagulls above wailed their mournful cry, and it was the loneliest sound in the world.

"I'll make you proud of me, Morgan," the voices in my head whispered.

And I could take it no more.

I stepped out into the sea.

I stepped out as a woman with the spectre of a thousand bad decisions at her heels in a burst of furious kinetic energy, and bent myself low as I surged forward, holding out my arms as if to embrace the night, and my feet left the earth, I had finally escaped gravity, and I sailed over the edge of the cliff as the Folly watched from behind, a silent, black tomb for two men who should have known better, who should have behaved better, and for a second I was flying, flying like the seagulls, and then I disappeared from view, a stone dropped into the ocean.

If only the tide was out, I thought, even as I screamed and fell.

And then there was only water.

TWENTY-ONE

A death tourist saved my life, ironically.

A group of them had been holding a macabre candlelit vigil in the roped-off cave when they'd heard me scream and fall into the water. They'd made a human chain, grabbing me before the violent swell had a chance to shred me against the rocks that lurked under the surface of the sea. It was lucky that the tide was up at its highest point, where it all but kissed the floor of the cave ledge. Any lower, and nobody would have been able to reach me.

I stayed in hospital for a while. My body recovered faster than my brain did.

Afterward, I didn't go back to the Folly. I wound up in a woman's shelter until I figured things out. In time, I got a job, as I was now free to do. I found a small, run-down cottage just up the coast. The rent was only affordable because it was in such a terrible state, but I didn't mind. I figured I could do it up myself, over time, and the landlord, an elderly gent who lived a few miles away, might knock my rent down if he saw what I was doing for the place.

Not long after I moved in, a solicitor's letter found its way through my letterbox.

Inside the envelope lay a photograph of my mother, smiling, a grin I rarely saw as a child. Next to her, a younger version of the man I last saw lying in a bundle at the bottom of the Folly stairs as I stepped casually over him. He had hair in this picture.

Between them, my parents, in their arms, a small, wriggling, blurry shape.

Me.

He'd been allowed to visit once, just after I'd been born. Then Mum and Dad had moved away, started a new life, kept me from him.

I wondered how hard that must have been, to have made a mistake, so young, so very young, and then be denied any way of making up for it.

I wondered about my dad, rearing me as his own so my Mum did not have to live life as a shunned woman, stigmatised for having a baby after a one-night stand, ostracised in the way that women with babies with no father present were in those days, even though you would have thought society had moved on by then, but it hadn't, and they had both known it. They had both wanted to give me a good life, and they had. Born of love, Dad had said, and he'd meant it. I strove to remember that in my darkest moments. I strove to remember the good times, because it had all, I knew, when I lay awake at night staring at the ceiling, been for me. All of it.

All of it had been for me.

I understood that.

But it didn't make it any easier to bear.

Twenty-Two

Another day. I was waiting for a door to open. It was the front door of a well-cared-for terraced cottage just outside Newquay. It overlooked the sea, as a house should. I felt that to my core. Every human being should have the right to open their eyes and curtains and see the ocean, hear the sound of millions of tons of water moving, restless as a sleeping giant.

The door opened, and a woman who was roughly my age, or near enough, stood behind it. Simultaneously, we held our hands to our mouths: it was as if I were standing before a mirror.

Only it was not a mirror. It was my sister, or my half-sister, and we looked just like each other.

"Come here," she said, tears streaming down her

face.

She smelled familiar and yet not, and it was heady and disorienting. We held each other on the doorstep, one in, one out, and I understood with enormous relief that no matter what happened from this point forward, I was still anchored, I still had a harbour.

After a moment or two, we broke apart.

"Well, come in, then," she said gruffly. I could tell she didn't like to make a fuss, and I refrained from telling her we were alike in that sense. "I made apple pie, it should still be warm."

It was warm, and good. A different recipe to Mum's, but maybe a better one. Something about the pastry ignited my taste buds. Was it love? Maybe. I knew as soon as I set eyes on my sister that I would love her. I felt the same emotion from her: it was in her smile.

When my bowl was empty, she said something I could never have anticipated.

"He left you some money, you know." There was no malice or jealousy in her as she imparted this information. Rather, she seemed pleased for me.

I blinked in shock.

"Why? I thought...I thought he was..."

"Poor? Depends on your definition, I suppose. A fisherman's salary varies year to year. But he was prudent. He saved from the day you were born."

I swallowed back tears. "How much?" With anyone

else, it would have been a tacky question. With her, I instinctively knew I was on safe ground.

She smiled, a brilliant, broad smile with nothing but love inside it.

"Enough," she said.

Twenty-Three

A different ocean. Warmer, turquoise blue. Instead of a stern man-made harbour, there were impressive boulders and rocks, a sweeping variety of trees adorning a bay that was one of the most picturesque on the island of Corfu. The secluded cove was blanketed by an expanse of luscious green that came down a steep incline to meet an idyllic, crescent-moon-shaped beach at the bottom. In the middle of the bay, a large hotel: tastefully designed, squat and long, distinguished by the usual repeating archways, which I was learning was typical of modern Greek seaside architecture. Recently redecorated, the building had none of the shabby tiredness that characterised so many British seaside hotels. Everything here was sleek and sharp and new and fresh, and I hadn't realised how much I had needed that until now. Fresh start, fresh paint: it all went hand in hand.

Further along the coast, a small town—or maybe village was more accurate—huddled by the water's edge. Dotted up the hillside, I saw the odd holiday home, commanding incredible views of the ocean and all else that lay below. I couldn't quite see the appeal of living up there when you had the sea right here to swim in, but I imagined it was more peaceful than the hotel.

From my vantage point in the brilliant blue, bobbing up and down gently as waves rocked me like a mother rocking a baby to sleep, the bay, the hotel, the people within: none of it looked real. It looked like a scene made with models, toys. It was amazing how a different perspective changed things in a person's life. I could get an understanding out here, with my body weight cradled by the ocean, that a lot of the things I had been so troubled by recently were insignificant, really. Terrible things, painful things, to be sure, but with perspective, I was learning that it was all part of being one of the many crawling tiny people who lived on the earth. Not that I thought for one second it made us all equal, the sum of our experiences, but it helped me, just as it helped me to stare at the ocean and imagine the great beasts who sculled around in the depths. I once again had a place in the scheme of things, and that place was determined by factors above and beyond my control. Once I learned to accept that—which was, admittedly, an easier task while I was surrounded by such idyllic scenery—things had become much more tolerable.

I watched the people, the small model people, milling about: playing bat and ball, swimming, slowly cooking themselves under a strong Mediterranean sun, showering, drinking beer, staring at phones, reading books. I heard small children crying and saw couples holding hands. I saw sweating hotel employees clad in black rushing about, tending to the needs of richer people who didn't appreciate for one moment how hard the staff had to work: they were on holiday, after all, uncomfortable truths were not part of the itinerary. Question any one of them about it, and they would have said, "But we're contributing to the local economy, right?" and that would have been that. People would say anything to make their own existence more comfortable, I knew. That was a truth the ocean could not hold the weight of, not fully.

That being said, I didn't mind the people, for once. It was technically off-season on the island, but that didn't seem to matter now that travel restrictions had been lifted and holidaymakers were allowed to fly once again. To begin with, I'd been horribly anxious with so many new neighbours to coexist alongside, but it didn't take me long to settle in, find a rhythm. I hadn't realised how isolated I'd been in the Folly with Dad until I left it. How much I'd missed the general noise of conversation, of human interaction. I still got tired of people very quickly, especially wailing babies and brattish kids, but I learned to rest a lot, which helped. Resting had never been something I'd been very good at, until now.

Swimming in the ocean every day helped, too.

At first, I was nervous. The sea had no longer felt like it belonged to me, not after Cornwall. Not after the big, cold, wet explosion of that night. It had been too wild there, in the sea. I had felt the most vulnerable I'd ever felt. A tiny ant on the tumultuous, wind-churned surface of a huge planet, alone, exposed, my own end inevitable. It had not mattered that I was a strong swimmer and always had been. None of that mattered if the sea decided to swallow you whole.

Here, though, it felt safer somehow. The water was still choppy, meaning you could never quite relax without being hit by a sprightly breaker when you least expected it, and there was a definite undertow, but nothing a good, strong breaststroke couldn't fight against. I had gotten into the habit of three swims a day, timed for when most of the other hotel guests were eating their meals, although there was ample room for us all.

After the first few days, I conquered my fears and learned not to hug the shoreline, venturing further and further out into the bay. In doing so, I rediscovered the intense sensation of freedom that could come from being surrounded by so much water. I felt myself grow stronger, day by day, as the sun freckled my face and my skin turned from white, to pink, to a subtle shade of tan.

Today, I intended to push myself. I was going to swim as far as the yellow buoys which marked the recommended limit, and, if I felt brave enough, perhaps even a little further. There were no lifeguards here to shout at me, and I wanted to know what it felt like. To be floating in the deep, with all those giant sea creatures I'd fantasised about back home slowly passing beneath. Were there sharks? Dolphins? Huge fish? I didn't know, and didn't care. I just wanted to be out there, reinforcing my place in the ecosystem again.

I struck out into the bay as usual, and swam until I had crossed the first trench, after which a sandbar striped the floor of the ocean yellow beneath me, raising the seabed up. I always liked reaching this little strip, for the sea crashed a different colour out here, and it meant I could put my feet down for a moment and rest. It was warmer in this part, too, shallower.

I lay on my back, letting my feet bob to the surface, and windmilled my hands, pivoting my body until I was facing inland and could get a good look, past my toes, at the coastline, which was dramatic, with small jagged peaks and gentle green slopes all jostling for attention against the sky, which was, as it had been in Cornwall on good days, a deep, abiding blue, decorated with wispy white clouds. There were palm trees down at ground level that the hotel had no doubt planted, and again, they reminded me of Cornwall.

But everything reminded me of Cornwall, whether I wanted it to or not.

I floated, and I thought about Mum. Her comfortable bones. Mine were comfortable now, too, as my body was held aloft by the water. No pressure, no gravity, not the kind that weighed me down, at any rate.

Are you at peace now? I wondered, water lapping in my ears.

Something sharp and scratchy stung my thigh. I yelped and floundered, catching a glimpse of a small fish swimming away. Amused, I laughed at myself for being scared after a tiny fish bite, but I still headed back to the shore. One bite was enough. Only an idiot would stick around to be bitten more than once.

I emerged from the sea clumsily, for the waves at the shore line were powerful enough to make me stagger, and plodded my way up the beach to a sun lounger, my feet burning on the boiling hot sand. Collapsing onto the lounger, I let my body dry in the heat, enjoying the sensation. It was very rare that you could air dry back home. It was too humid, for one thing, down in the

West. You ended up exchanging one type of wet for another.

Propping myself up, I surveyed the beach around me, the slight sense of unease that the fish bite had aroused dissipating.

To my left, I noted a family of three, sitting close to each other, two parents in their forties and a boy who looked to be about nine or ten years old. He really should have been in school, but he looked happy enough where he sat, sandwiched between them. They were playing cards in the shade of their umbrella, and the boy was cheating, slapping down his hand gleefully and shouting "Uno!" while the parents rolled their eyes and smiled indulgently.

To my right, two empty sun loungers, then a woman in a baseball cap, holding a book up above her face to shade it from the sun.

My mouth went dry.

Her other hand worked busily around and around in the air near her head.

She was twirling a strand of hair around her fingers.

I couldn't stop looking, mesmerised by the thick, glossy rope of chestnut that slid in and around and through her tanned digits.

The woman was not only twirling her hair. She was doing it exactly the same way Mum used to.

She lowered her book, scanned her own surroundings. This was what people did on the beach. They watched each other covertly.

She saw me staring at her.

I didn't even try to hide the fact that I was watching.

I knew who she really was.

I wasn't afraid anymore.

She smiled at me, then went back to sunbathing, book down on her chest, face turned upward, baseball cap tilted now to shade her eyes. Music trickled out of large headphones covering her ears. She turned it up a notch or two, so I could make out the tune, even from where I lay.

"Waterloo."

I identified this in the same moment I realised I had my own hand up to the side of my head, endlessly fiddling with a single strand of wet, salt-washed hair, which had grown long enough to play with, like grass growing from the roots, covering a multitude of sins.

About the Author

Gemma Amor is the Bram Stoker and British Fantasy Award nominated author of *Dear Laura*, *Six Rooms*, *White Pines* and the *Full Immersion* (Angry Robot, Sept 2022). She is the co-creator of *Calling Darkness*, a comedy-horror podcast starring Kate Seigel (Haunting of Hill House, Midnight Mass) and many of her works have been adapted into audio drama format by the multi-million download horror anthology show *The NoSleep Podcast*, who she has also toured with. She is also a voice actor and illustrator, and is based in Bristol, in the U.K.